At what cost will Daniel and Mary Anna's dream become reality?

The noise of the children at the supper table covered the silence between husband and wife, but there was no avoiding going to bed together. They were very formal with one another, strangers sharing a bed.

Mary Anna tried hard to get over her anger, but she couldn't let go of it. Daniel left her alone, waiting for his sweet, sensible wife to come back to him.

She was still mad as he prepared to go. "It isn't safe, Daniel. I need you here." The words came out of tight lips.

Quietly he turned from his horse and said, "I'm sorry. But I have to do this. And I'm sorry you don't understand." He leaned down and kissed her still mouth.

She wanted to cry out, "Stay, I love you, I can't bear to see you go, please!" But her lips wouldn't move. She watched him mount up and leave with his men.

LINDA HERRING is the mother of four grown children and the wife of a minister. *Dreams Fulfilled* is the last of Linda Herring's trilogy based on the lives of her great-great-grandparents. Linda lives in Texas, and has enjoyed the opportunity to learn her family's heritage as she researched these books.

Books by Linda Herring

HEARTSONG PRESENTS
HP49—Yesterday's Tomorrows
HP72—Song of Captivity
HP148—Dreams of the Pioneers
HP163—Dreams of Glory

Dreams
Fulfilled

Linda Herring

The Thornton Saga

Heartsong Presents

For Mary Anna Thornton Smith
who turned back the pages of time
and showed me my history.

A note from the Author:
*I love to hear from my readers! You may write to me at
the following address:*   **Linda Herring**
Author Relations
P.O. Box 719
Uhrichsville, OH 44683

ISBN 1-55748-931-9

DREAMS FULFILLED

Cover illustration by Kathy Arbuckle.

one

Barton Springs, Texas
1868

The prairie sky was marbled with blues and oranges. Wisps of white feathered cirrus clouds curled around the deep purples of the sunset. Raucous mockingbirds strove to outdo each other in announcing the setting of the sun.

Daniel could hear the soft singing of the small stream out behind the cabin, and the smell of Mary Anna's supper teased his taste buds. The babble of their five children blended with their mother's firm commands.

He tipped his rawhide-bottomed chair back against the rude logs of the cabin he and Mary Anna had built the year before with help from their friends, the Wests. Turning his head to the east, he could see the Wests' cabin on the other side of the communal garden Mary Anna and Virginia had planted.

The sudden nickering of horses in the corral made Daniel sit up, alerting all his senses. Any sound of disruption with the horses was cause for concern. They were the prime target of the renegade Comanches, better than gold or silver.

Many of the Comanches and other tribes were off the reservations since the end of the war. Few troops were available to contain them, and the Indians were taking their revenge on the settlers who had torn the land from them.

The startled sound of the horses quieted, and Daniel listened for a minute more. All sounded well, so he slowly eased himself back into his chair. Fear for his horses was replaced by thoughts of the upcoming cattle roundup and the fall drive to market.

When I first came to Texas, people told me it was a land flowing with milk and honey, and so it has been. But they didn't mention how hard it would be to collect on that promise, he thought wryly. *Still, the Lord has provided for us up to this point. He won't let us down now.*

Two cowboys Daniel had hired came strolling up from the bunkhouse for supper. Mary Anna had invited them to eat with the family. Daniel hoped it wouldn't be too long before there were too many cowboys to feed, and he'd have to hire a cook just for the men.

"Howdy, Mr. Thornton," said Coleman. His ferocious black mustache barely moved when he spoke, giving him a solemn look even when he was smiling. His sidekick, Toad, stuck his thumbs inside the pockets of his heavy denim pants and added his greeting. Daniel stood up and the three men entered the house, where Mary Anna was waiting to serve the meal.

Mary Anna always had to hide a smile when Toad took off his hat to her. His hair resembled a red haystack, no matter how much water he put on it when he combed through it. And his freckles belonged on the fair skin that came with the red hair. He looked to be about seventeen. Coleman was in his mid twenties. They looked very young to thirty-one-year-old Mary Anna, but they didn't looked untried.

The noise and confusion of four adults and five children finding their places around the supper table quieted when Daniel paused to say grace. As the baked beans, roast, biscuits, gravy, and canned corn from the last year's harvest circled the table, all conversation focused on the upcoming roundup.

During a break in the talk, fourteen-year-old Tump cleared his throat. "Papa?" he asked hesitantly. "I work with the horses and cattle every day. Can't I go on the roundup with you this year? I know I could help. Please?"

Daniel looked at his oldest son in surprise, then glanced across the table at Mary Anna. "Son," he said gently, "I do appreciate how you've taken on responsibilities this past year and been a real help to both me and your mama. That's why I have to say no. While I'm gone, your mama's going to rely on you to take care of the animals that we leave behind and to set an example for your brothers and sister. I'm depending on you to be the man of the family while I'm gone. Do you understand?"

The light of anticipation died from Tump's eyes, and they looked suspiciously wet as he quickly looked down at his plate. "Yes, sir," he whispered.

"Tump," Mary Anna added, "I know that this is a big disappointment to you, that waiting to take part in big adventures can seem to take forever, but I can't tell you what a comfort it will be to me to know you are here during all those months your papa will be gone."

Her oldest son gave her a tremulous smile, but Mary Anna knew it would take some weeks before Tump had adjusted to this latest disappointment.

Supper over, the men went outdoors to continue settling the details of the roundup. Mary Anna was cleaning up the supper things and getting the children tucked into bed when she heard a soft knock on the open door.

"Evening, Mary Anna." Virginia West was skinny as a shadow, as though honed down to her limit, yet she was getting a healthy glow about her with good food and Mary Anna's companionship. "Got my young ens tucked in.

Thought we could talk a little." She helped herself to a cup of coffee from the pot on the back of the stove and settled herself in a chair by the kitchen table. "Caleb wanted to talk with the men, too, about the roundup."

Mary Anna's eyes gleamed with mischief. "Wouldn't it be fun to go with them?"

Virginia was visibly shocked. "It would not! I would never, ever even think of going on that trip with a bunch of men and horses and cattle. I'll stay here in my cozy cabin, thank you."

"But it would be such an adventure," Mary Anna sighed. "Tump was asking if he could go this year, and while of course he can't, I must say I sympathize with his desire. I've never been that far north before. I think they've decided on the Kansas railhead. I've heard it's a big city. Bigger than any I've seen. Think of the shopping and the restaurants and hotels."

"And they'll all be filled with filthy cowboys who haven't had a decent bath or change of clothes since they left home, and they'll probably all be looking for a good time. The only women in that town are most likely the kind we don't talk about." Virginia looked at her friend suspiciously. "You're reading those romantic books again, aren't you?" she teased.

Mary Anna colored slightly. "Daniel found an old *Godey's Magazine* for me in town last week."

"And you didn't tell me?" Virginia jumped up from the table. "Where is it? I want to see the latest fashions." She tried to look stern. "And there was a romance story in it, too, wasn't there?"

Mary Anna clasped her hands. "Oh, it is so romantic and sad. I cried and cried after I finished it. I was going to give it to you as soon as I was done with it," she added contritely.

"You didn't cry," Virginia said flatly. "You never cry unless you're happy."

"But I was happy. The ending of the story was so beautiful." She opened one of her brass-bound trunks and took out the magazine, smoothing its cover with her hand. Then she gave it to her friend.

Virginia's grin was broad. "I'll give it back to you when I'm finished," she promised.

Mary Anna joined her at the table with her own cup of coffee. She sighed as she lifted the cup to her lips.

"Why the sigh?"

"I was thinking of all the work that has to be done between now and the time the men come back from the drive. The Land of Milk and Honey is there for the taking, but my, what a price must be paid."

"Caleb saw Comanche signs out on the north pasture yesterday," Virginia said softly. "It's just a matter of time, you know."

"I know. I have everything ready here in the cabin if they decide to hit the house."

"No one knows what the Comanches think. If we're real lucky, they'll take only the stock." Virginia sipped carefully from the blue-bordered china cup.

"It won't be luck, Virginia. It will be God's mercy. I don't believe in luck. I think the Almighty has a plan for all of us. We may not understand it or even like it, but it isn't luck. And it isn't written in stone. Different people make all kinds of decisions that somehow affect us. Then the Lord brings good out of it to accomplish His ultimate goal for us."

Virginia's face turned a delicate shade of gray, and her

jaw tensed. "It's His will about all this killing and my babies dying?" she asked in a rough voice.

"No, but He was there when all that was happening, and He's used it to make you the woman you are today. A fine woman, strong and wise. You are able to sympathize and care for other women who have suffered as you have, because you've been there." Mary Anna patted her friend's rough hand. "God's love and strength have brought us through all our trials to make us what we are today. Think of all the women who are not nearly as smart as we are," she added with a rueful chuckle.

"I'm glad I know the things I know, but that doesn't mean I want to go through them again," Virginia said, a tiny mist of tears forming in her eyes.

"I know. But we will if we have to. And we will survive it." Mary Anna held Virginia's hand briefly and gave it a loving squeeze. "We're in better shape here than we have been the entire time we've been living in Texas."

Virginia dried her eyes on the hem of her apron. "That's true. We have more men to defend us with Toad and Coleman. And our cabins are close together. The new bunkhouse is right there." She laughed out loud. "You should have seen the looks on Toad and Coleman's faces when Daniel asked them to help finish building the bunkhouse. You know, it's against the code of the cowboy to do anything that can't be done from the back of a horse. Building isn't one of those things. Until Daniel agreed to pay them extra and reminded them the Comanches are going to want those horses, they wouldn't agree to help. I think it was Coleman who said he didn't want to be fighting the Indians out in the open, so they worked like slaves to get it done."

After their laughter died down, Mary Anna added, "I'm

sure glad I'm not married to a cowboy."

"But you are," Virginia argued.

"Nope. Daniel will have to work as a cowboy for a while, but he says he'll be a cattleman one day."

"Ah. The cattleman owns the ranch and the cowboys work it. Right?"

"Right."

"Then I guess I'm married to a cattleman, too!" Virginia laughed.

While the women talked in the warm kitchen, the "cattlemen" talked with their cowboys outside, under the trees in the swept front yard. Big branches swayed in the night air. April weather was notoriously fickle. Today had been a pleasantly warm day, and the breeze felt good.

Daniel and his neighbor, Caleb West, were determined to gather some of the stray cattle that roamed the Texas prairie. The animals had been abandoned by their owners for as many reasons as there were cows, and anyone willing to risk life and limb rounding them up and branding them could claim them. Then the animals would be taken to the railhead, where they would be sold.

"How many horses we got broke?" Caleb asked.

"Oh, maybe two dozen," Daniel answered.

"I'm breaking 'em as fast as I can," Toad said.

"You keep doing what you're doing. Breaking 'em faster isn't what I have in mind. I want them handled gentle. No rough stuff," Daniel said firmly. "Coleman, are you and Caleb going out tomorrow to drive those cows in from the south?"

"Yes, sir. I reckon I spotted about thirty head down there. We could use another hand."

"That'll leave the women only one man on the place. No offense, Toad, but there's a Comanche Moon coming up soon.

I can feel it in my bones that we're probably going to get hit. Cattle or horses, I don't know. You get those cows up here to the ranch into that cattle pen as fast as a greased pig. Two men out there isn't any more safe than one man on the place."

"You'll be adding more cowboys soon?" Coleman asked.

"I will. Like to find some honest men who'll work for their wage."

"Don't everyone?" interjected Caleb with a laugh.

"Mr. West and me'll swing by Stephenville and leave word at the mercantile store. That'll spread the news," Coleman offered. Stephenville was about twelve miles southwest.

"That'll lose you two days of getting to those cows," Daniel worried. "But we need the help. Do it—but don't tell Mrs. Thornton, or you'll have a list of things as long as your arm that she needs from the mercantile store." Chuckling, he rose and stretched in the glow of the moon.

"I used to love to see that old moon get big and fat like it was so heavy it would fall from the sky," said Caleb. "Now I get butterflies in my stomach every time it gets full."

"I guess we all do. They may not wait that long, so keep your eyes and ears peeled for any signs." Daniel yawned.

"I've already spotted some today on the north pasture. Horse tracks. Unshod ponies. Better sleep with your rifle for a while."

Toad and Coleman headed for the bunkhouse, while Daniel and Caleb headed for the cabin. "You best tell the women," Daniel said.

"Virginia knows. She's prob'ly already told Mary Anna."

Later that night, Daniel took his own advice and kept the rifle handy as he slept. He knew Mary Anna was sleeping as lightly as he was. *I'll look for the day when I can sleep the sleep of the righteous the whole night through. It's coming,* he promised himself, *it's coming. Patience. The Lord is on guard, too.*

২

The next few days were a flurry of activity as cows were brought in and put protestingly into the cattle pens. Four more men drifted in to help with the roundup and brand the cattle with the Thornton brand: the Diamond T. It honored Daniel's promise—made way back when he and Mary Anna first came west—to buy Mary Anna a huge diamond as big as the stars.

"I wouldn't know what to do with a big diamond," she'd argued with him. "I'd rather have another woman to come in and help with the chores."

"You know I can't afford that," he'd countered. "I need men for the drive."

A little sourly she'd conceded, "I'm sorry—I got my lists mixed up." But she knew he was right.

Most of the men wouldn't see their money until the end of the drive when the cattle were sold at market value. Until then, food had to be provided for them, and Mary Anna used her experience from cooking in her father's hotel as a young lady to provide large quantities of delicious food for the hard-working men.

Toad and Coleman shared their small bunkhouse until it was crowded, and the rest of the men slept in the barn.

"This place is beginning to look like a real ranch," Mary Anna told Daniel. "Cowboys everywhere I look."

"I hope the Comanches are looking, too. Maybe they won't want to take on so big a band of white men."

But instead of the Indians, the army came riding in.

"Lieutenant Mooreland," barked the cocky young man who sat on a prancing red roan. "I'm here to buy horses."

His arrogance was irritating to Daniel, but the possibility of getting cash from the government kept Daniel from making the tart reply perched on the tip of his tongue. Instead he deliberately withheld the customary invitation for his visitor to get down off his horse and simply asked, "How many horses did you have in mind?"

Ignoring Daniel's rudeness, the lieutenant got off his horse and dusted his clothes. "That depends entirely on the quality of the animals," he responded.

The blue of the lieutenant's uniform did nothing to smooth Daniel's ruffled feathers. *A blue-belly is a blue-belly,* said his Southern heart.

The Union's hand had been hard on the beaten South. Taxes were unjustly high and the few government men Daniel had had the misfortune of dealing with had been complete scoundrels. Talk in town was rough tongued against Reconstruction policies.

"Been here long, Lieutenant Mooreland?" Daniel asked casually.

The man blushed slightly. "A month," he replied.

"Then you should know that the horses I sell are good. That's the only kind I sell. Kind of a point of honor with me," he drawled.

"Honor for a reb," one of the men in the patrol snickered. "That's a good one."

Daniel felt his blood rise. Silently he led the men to the corral, where Coleman and some of the hands were working with the horses.

The lieutenant was clearly pleased with what he saw. "I can use ten. I'll give you ten dollars a piece."

Daniel was tempted to ask for fifteen dollars just because of how he was feeling toward the government, but the lieutenant had offered a fair price. Daniel signed the requisition, wondering if the money would ever actually be paid.

"We'll be back in a week or so. I'll bring you the money," Lieutenant Mooreland promised.

Daniel nodded, biting back sarcastic words about the worth of government promises.

"Any trouble with the Indians?" the lieutenant asked as he remounted.

"Just signs lately." He chose not to elaborate.

"You're lucky if you didn't lose any horses or get anyone killed. The farm a few miles from here lost all their stock and had one man killed. Probably Santana's work." He sighed. "We do what we can." He adjusted the ornate saber at his side. "We'll get them eventually. We got Nocona, and we'll get that squirt Quannah Parker, too."

"I believe that was J. H. Cureton and Captain Rip Ford who got Nocona," Daniel said quietly.

"Spangler had twenty men in there, too," was the brief reply.

"Took almost a hundred men to kill him. Parker isn't going to be any easier." He eyed the small patrol. "Hope you don't meet up with him on this trip. He learned everything from his father."

Angrily Lieutenant Mooreland replied, "He'd have one big fight on his hands if we did meet." Without another word, the man and his patrol began herding the horses away from the corral.

"You're a prime target with all those horses," Daniel warned the retreating men's backs. In spite of his anger, he didn't wish the men dead. Frightened out of their haughtiness, yes, but not dead.

As the lieutenant and his men headed out, Coleman

walked over to his boss. "The Indians will take the uppity notions out of them the first go-round," he told Daniel solemnly. "Nothing like a war whoop to take the starch out of a man's underwear."

Daniel laughed in spite of the painful truth of the statement. "Well, men, we're richer now if we get paid. Guess I'll be able to pay your wages this month."

That brought a big smile from the hands.

"Course the downside is that we need more horses broken." He threw a small salute toward Toad. "Go to it, boy, and take one of the new men with you. You can show him what to do."

Toad's chest swelled a little with pride at being made the head man of the team by his boss.

❧

Daniel came in to supper that night exhausted. His greeting wasn't as warm as usual. When he sat down at the table, he simply prayed out of habit, "For what we are about to receive, O Lord, make us truly grateful," and fell to eating.

When Daniel had eaten enough to ease his hunger and tiredness, he looked at Mary Anna. She had been silent through the meal. "You must be as tired as I am," he said carefully. Mary Anna's temper had moderated through the years, but Daniel would never forget those tempestuous early days of their marriage.

"I am."

"I'll get you some help as soon as I can," he promised, eager to lift her spirits.

"I know." She sat down beside him at the table. "It's just that everything is for the ranch right now, and I still have a dirt floor." She burst into a flood of tears that totally unnerved Daniel. Mary Anna never cried unless she was happy.

Clumsily he stood and took her in his arms. "I'll put in floors for you, if that's what you want. You only have to ask me."

"And a cellar," she sniffed.

"All right." He smoothed her hair back from her face. "Anything else?"

"Windows. I need windows so I can see the lovely spring," she sniffed. "I'll need the fresh air for the baby," she added softly.

It took a moment for the message to sink in. "The baby. A baby. That's what all this is about. You're going to have another baby! Oh, Mary Anna, I'm thrilled! When?" He held her closer.

"Early January, I think."

"I'll get everything done for you and the new baby before I go on the drive in the fall. You'll be as snug as a big old black bear sleeping off the winter. All of us will be." The laughter in his eyes drifted to his mouth in the form of a big smile. "I love you, Mary Anna Garland Thornton. More and more every year."

"And I love you, too, Daniel Robert Thornton. Thank you for fixing up the cabin into a real house."

"Anything for my love," he promised, knowing that it would be a struggle to find the time to get the project finished. He knew better than to ask the cowboys to help, and he needed them doing cowboy's work anyway.

The next day, Daniel confided in Caleb about his problem.

Caleb looked at Daniel with great sympathy. "She's going to have a baby, isn't she?" he guessed wisely with a shake of his head.

"Yes, and I'm happy about that." In spite of his words,

Daniel looked miserable.

"I know. But that's when they start wanting the durndest things. Well, the onliest thing I know to do is fer you and me to get busy so we can git on with the cattle business. We've got to keep our wives happy, else we're doing all this ranching business for nothing."

With the two of them working and their older boys helping, it didn't take too long to dig a cellar with a hinged door over it, set in new puncheon floors. They put in small windows with shutters on either side. The windows could be raised for airing the cabin, and the shutters could either be partially closed for firing a rifle during a raid or shut up tight for the coming winter winds.

When the work was finally done, Mary Anna was ecstatic over the improvements to her home. She pranced around the room and positively glowed with pride.

"This is a real home. Something to be proud of. Oh, thank you two for all this." Much to Caleb's surprise she grabbed both of the men around the neck and bumped them together with her big hug.

As the men walked outside Mary Anna's hearing, Caleb said glumly, "Well, you know what else this means."

Daniel sighed and nodded his head. "Yup. Your cabin next, right?"

"You're a man wise beyond your years in the ways of women," said Caleb as he reached for his tools and headed toward his cabin.

The raw smell of the beautiful wood on her floor and windows was like the fragrance of the forest after a cooling rain, and Mary Anna sat in her rocker for a little while and let it flow around her. Then she smiled as she heard the familiar sound of hammering and sawing coming from Virginia's home. "We have the best husbands in the world," she reflected as she laid her head back against the rocker and smiled and smiled.

That evening Coleman and Toad were invited for supper so that plans for the drive could be finalized. After the meal, Caleb joined them, and the serious planning began. Coleman used a piece of brown wrapping paper to draw a rough map, indicating the general trails known to him.

"I've rode with Goodnight and Loving." Lest they think him a braggart, he added, "I wasn't their trail boss, but I kept my eyes and ears open. I know that way. We wuz on the trail about two months. Guess we went close to seven hundred miles. Long miles, too. The trick is to get there first. But," he added, "you have some flooding in the rivers.

"You know we're going to have trouble with the Indians and rustlers. After that, all you have to worry about is having water on them long stretches. There's been some talk that the Kansas farmers don't want us bringing our cattle in because they claim that they cause some kind of fever. Personally, I doubt that. Probably getting it from the Indians. We'll need more men, depending on how ever many cows we push."

"Before the war I ran a small herd with Wylie, a friend of mine, to Palo Pinto," said Daniel. "We did it with just four of us, but it was a small herd. We drove them to Palo Pinto to put them in with another herd. Now I want a big herd, and I plan to take it all the way." A ripple of excitement passed from one man to the other.

What is it, Mary Anna wondered as she listened to the men talk, *that pulls men to take on such a job?* It meant possible wealth for her and Daniel, but the wages for the cowboys could easily be lost in the many temptations of the trail towns. Still, there sat Toad and Coleman with vibrations of excitement running through them. She tried to recapture the feelings of adventure she had expressed earlier to Virginia, but in the reality of talking about the drive, she, too, was grateful she could stay in her home. *Two months,* she thought with dismay.

"How many horses do you think we'll need for the remuda?" Daniel asked Coleman.

"It's best to take about eight or ten for each man. Lots of things can happen to a mount. Seven hundred miles can wear out a lot of horseflesh."

"We can get the horses, no problem there. Finding the men may be another thing. The war seems to have used up lot of them," Daniel added a little bitterly.

"You've started the word out. The men will find you. Choosing the good ones will be the tricky part," Coleman assured him. "You do understand they will call you captain because you're the one with the money invested."

Daniel's eyebrows rose. "Captain? I never thought to be called a captain at this late date."

"Cattle drive is a lot like an army maneuver. Takes teamwork and good strong leadership," Coleman assured him.

Coleman was just beginning to discuss the dangers of a stampede when Mary Anna decided she had heard enough. When she rose and began tidying up, the three guests hastily excused themselves. Caleb walked back over to his cabin, and Coleman and Toad headed toward the bunkhouse.

Quiet descended on their home. Daniel went to Mary Anna and wrapped his arms around her tiny figure. "Too much man talk tonight?" He kissed her softly. "You won't mind so much when I buy that diamond and build that mansion for you."

"I think I already have that mansion," she sighed. "I'm just worrying about who will defend it from the Indians while you're off playing cowboy."

"Remember? I'm the cattleman. They're the cowboys." He helped himself to a kiss.

In spite of herself, she felt the familiar stirrings beginning. "You're terrible," she breathed, even as she returned his kiss.

"I know. All us cattle barons are like that."

Later as she lay in their bed, she thought about the baby. Her smile was broad as she decided it would be a girl this time. Another girl for her. She loved her three sons and was proud of them. They would help make the ranch dream continue. But the girls were hers. Companions. Dear friends when they grew up. A little sister for Betty. She would name her Annah. And then there would be grandchildren. . . . She fell asleep before she could plan the rest of her life.

two

As the cattle and horse herds began to grow, so did Daniel's fear of attacks from Indians and rustlers. The men riding night guard had scared off a couple would-be cattle thieves. But the Indians had been strangely quiet. It made Daniel nervous. He was anxious to get on the trail, yet he knew he would be more exposed than ever to attack.

Mary Anna knew he was deeply worried. One night after the children were in bed and she and Daniel were sitting at the kitchen table discussing the day, she said, "Daniel, I sense you aren't easy about something."

Daniel stared into his coffee cup, watching the lantern light reflected in the black liquid. After a pause, he admitted, "You're right. No matter what I do, I know our herd is vulnerable to attack, and there's nothing much more I can do to protect it."

Quietly she said, "I think you need to spend a lot more time in prayer. No one on earth can keep your herd together all the way to Kansas. Give your worries to the Lord and let Him take care of things."

Daniel rubbed his index finger around the rim of his cup. Finally, he put his cup down on the table and stood up. "Mary Anna, love, I need to go out and do me some talking with the Lord. Why don't you go ahead and get some sleep? I'll be joining you in a bit."

As he headed toward the door, Mary Anna rushed over and gave him a reassuring hug. Her gentle smile was the last thing he saw as he closed the door behind him. Daniel prayed long and hard that night under the starry sky before he went to bed. Looking at the stars thrown across the black heavens like tiny pieces of mirror put his life in perspective. "Lord," he prayed as he looked out over the land, "I'm not a man of many words, and You know I have trouble relying on anyone other than myself. I've depended on my wits and rifle to get me out of hard places most of my life. But I'm in a situation I can't handle on my own. Please give me peace of mind during the days and weeks ahead, and place Your protecting hand on our venture. Teach me how to follow Your leading and trust You. And more than anything, watch over Mary Anna and our children while I'm gone."

The next morning Daniel woke refreshed and eager for the day. Several more men drifted in asking about the drive. Daniel asked Coleman to screen the men and hire the ones he thought honest. "You'll be the trail boss," Daniel announced. "By the way," he grinned, "are you a praying man?"

"Yes, sir. I was saved during a run in with the Apaches a few years ago. Found me a town and a preacher and had myself baptized in the river. I'm pretty sure that's how I found this job. Praying for work."

Daniel noticed for the first time how Coleman's dark brown eyes gleamed from his face. Even the bushy eyebrows and mustache couldn't hide the glow.

"It's old Toad you need to work on, sir. He sure does need saving before we get to Kansas." Coleman laughed. "Even a saved man has to be careful up there."

"I know not all the men will be Christians, but choose the honest ones. I want to build a rock-hard reputation as an honest man. I plan to drive cattle to Kansas and anywhere else we can sell them. I want my reputation to precede me."

"I'll do the best I can, sir, but I can't guarantee you a bunch of knights in shining armor."

"I know," Daniel sighed.

The herd was fast swelling to fifteen-hundred head, and Daniel was even more certain that a raid was inevitable. So when a few nights later, he and Mary Anna were awakened by gunshots, he wasn't surprised. He and Mary Anna crawled out of bed, and Mary Anna heated some coffee on the stove. Guns at the ready, they anxiously hoped for news from the men who had been on guard—but they realized they could soon be facing an attack on their home.

About ten minutes later, they heard a horse galloping toward the cabin. "That's only one rider," Mary Anna whispered as she dimmed the lantern light. "Maybe we'll escape attack, at least for tonight."

Daniel peered cautiously through a crack in the shutters and breathed a sigh of relief when the rider came into view under the moonlight. Peterson was riding in with his report.

Daniel opened the door to the man, and Mary Anna passed him a cup of hot coffee.

"Got about ten head, Captain. No horses. I guess there was about fifteen of 'em. Not Comanches this time—Apaches. Things must not be goin' too well fer them either."

Daniel nodded with satisfaction. Maybe news that the Thornton Ranch was well guarded by watchful men would spread to other bands in the area, and the Indians would decide the ranch wasn't worth the trouble it brought. "Thanks, Peterson. Tell the men, well done."

After Peterson left to return to his duties, Daniel pulled Mary Anna into a fierce hug. "The Lord is answering my prayers already," he whispered. "His hand protected us and our children. Let's thank Him—and then get what little sleep we still can."

≥

Daniel had hired on several freedmen: blacks who had been freed by the war. They were good workers, glad to be able to choose their own boss and to roam where they pleased.

Caleb showed up with another freedman just at breakfast the next morning.

"Daniel Thornton, I want you to meet one of the best cooks in Texas. This here is Rabbit Washington Lincoln."

What Daniel saw first was a big wagon with pots and pans hanging off every side, clanging with a music all its own. Then he looked at the smiling man driving the covered wagon. The man jumped down and walked over to Daniel, taking off his slouch hat and extending his hand.

Daniel shook the man's hand and surveyed him. Lincoln was close to six feet, four inches tall and was as thin as a Lincoln rail. His hair was a mass of tightly kinked balls, and he looked to be around twenty. His clothes were old, but they were clean and neat.

"Howdy, Mr. Thornton." He held his hat in his hand respectfully. "I'm the best trail cook in Texas. My mammy was the number one cook on the plantation, and she taught me. I've been on two drives, and I can keep the men happy about the grub." Without taking a breath he added, "They call me Rabbit 'cause I can catch any one of 'em I can see and I make the best rabbit stew you ever wrapped your lips around."

"I kin testify to that myself," Caleb said. "I met Rabbit back during the war. He's a good man."

"Sounds like you're hired," Daniel grinned. "And this is your supply wagon?"

"Yes, sir. This here is a chuck wagon. Made it with the tailgate to drop down and make a table. Filled it with little drawers and cubbies for all my cooking things."

Daniel looked at the mules pulling the wagon. "You think

those two mules can make it all the way to Kansas?"

"Yes, sir. Savannah an' Alabama an' I have been together a long time. They kin pull a wagon all day long and not even be weary at the end of the day. They better than horses er oxes. They the best. I trained 'em myself."

As Rabbit rode off slowly to the barn, Daniel said, "Looks like it's all falling into place. I want to hurry up and get going. We should leave in two more days. Tell the men." Daniel grinned. "That'll be the easy part. Then we'll only have to tell our wives."

❧

Mary Anna took one look at Daniel's face and said, "I know. I can see it in your eyes. When?"

"Two days." He pulled her away from the sink and put his arms around her. Pain clouded his loving blue eyes. "Try not to be mad at me for leaving. The boys will still be here."

"An almost fourteen year old who's mad he can't go, a ten and a half year old, a two year old, and a babe in arms. The sight of those boys along with Betty and me ought to make old Ten Bears think twice before he comes to call." She paused, her eyes filling with tears. "I know you have to go. I just can't stand to think of something happening to you."

"I made it through the war." He grinned wickedly. "Who told me to pray about everything and that the Lord was in charge?"

She lightly hit him with the damp tea towel she was using to dry the dishes, then ducked her head. "I did. And I meant it." Suddenly she straightened up and looked him squarely in the eyes. "I made it through the war without you. This is only two months, more or less. You'll be back in time for the baby. Things are not that bad." She laid her head on his broad chest. "I miss you already." Then she reached up on tiptoe and kissed his mouth carefully. "I love you."

"I'll bring you some peppermint from Kansas," he smiled.

"That'll be wonderful. But don't forget the money, too," she teased back.

He looked at his petite wife, carrying their child, thought of the five other children, and made a decision. "I'll hire a man to stay on the place until we can make it back. He can be your handyman-guard and give Tump some help."

Her face brightened. "Yes, that would be wonderful! Make him big and burly. And smart."

Daniel flashed her a huge smile. "Just like me, huh?"

She pretended to throw the towel at him.

The next morning he rode toward Stephenville, colloquially called "Steamville," and took the two older boys with him. This was partially to assuage Tump for not getting to go on the drive and also to get his and Peter's views on anyone who might be staying with the family. They camped at Daniel's favorite place for the night. It was well sheltered, and they made a cold camp. Daniel felt they were relatively safe from unfriendly guests.

As he lay down on the ground in his bedroll, he remembered how much he hated to sleep on the ground. *And I have two months of this coming,* he complained to himself as he drifted off to sleep.

The next day he asked Charlie, the storekeeper in Stephenville, about a good man for staying at the ranch while he was gone.

Charlie scratched his round head, which amused Daniel, for the storekeeper had very few wisps of hair to bother him. "There's a young fellow kind of like you need around here. His ma owns the boarding house. But he don't strike me as the cowboy type. I can't think of anyone else."

Daniel thanked him and headed for the boarding house. It was a rude affair made of rough logs, and it served more as a hotel than a boarding house, for the people who stayed there rarely lingered more than a few days. He knocked politely on the slab of a door, which was answered by a careworn woman in her forties.

"Yes?"

"I'm looking for a young fellow who lives here."

"Ain't many of them around since the war," she said bitterly. "You work for the gov'nment?" Her eyes were suspicious.

"No. I might have a job for him."

She moved back from the door and invited him in to the common room which served as an eating area. "Someone here to see you, Thaddeus."

A mountain of a man stood up and turned around.

Daniel walked over to him quickly, for he also saw the empty pants leg and the crutch, and stuck out his hand as he introduced himself.

Thaddeus's eyes followed Daniel's to his stump. "Gettysburg," he said quietly. His voice was surprisingly soft for a man so large. He offered Daniel a chair and motioned Tump and Peter to a bench.

"Are you from around here?" Daniel asked politely. He was already doubtful about hiring a one-legged man. No matter how big or how nice Thaddeus might be, how could he possibly be able to protect Daniel's family or do any of the farm chores?

"This is my ma's boarding house," Thaddeus replied. "Lived here since the war."

Daniel liked the way Thaddeus looked him in the eye when they talked. There was nothing sly or evasive in his manner.

"I can see you know about fighting. Know anything about farming and ranching?"

"You offering me a job, Mr. Thornton?" Thaddeus asked.

"Possibly." He indicated the missing limb. "That slow you down much?"

"Not when I'm on a horse. And I'm quick with my crutch, too. It's a skill one must acquire as soon as possible."

"You talk like a schoolmaster."

"I did some of that before the war. Not much call for it now. Besides, most people don't like a one-legged man around to remind them about the war—especially now that the Union men are running things and they realize that I fought on the other side." His eyes shone like a blackbird's wing, and he was clean shaven and well-groomed, even though his clothes were shabby.

"I know how to read," Peter added helpfully.

"Good for you, boy. Keep up with it. Knowledge will always serve you well."

Daniel was liking what he saw more and more. "You appear to be in good health."

"I'm strong—especially my arms, what with carrying all this long body of mine around."

Daniel briefly described the circumstances he faced.

"I'm alone except for Ma. Reckon you could do without me for a few months, Ma?" he asked the woman hovering in the background.

"You going to pay him with real money?" she asked.

"Yes, ma'am. When I get back from the drive."

"You really going to try to take them longhorns through all them attacking thieves?" Skepticism was clearly marked on her face.

"Been done before," Daniel said easily. He turned back to Thaddeus. "Well? You want a job?"

"First good offer I've had since I got back. You just say when." His smile was pleasant, and the arrangements were quickly completed.

After a quick stop at the store for supplies, Daniel and the boys headed back toward home, talking about their experiences in town.

Tump said thoughtfully, "Papa, he seems so sad, even though he did smile."

"He's been through a lot, son. Time will ease the sadness."

Mary Anna was pleased someone had been found, but withheld her complete approval until she met the man. Tump put in a good word for him, as did Peter, and that made her feel somewhat better.

The grueling work of collecting the herd of longhorns and mustangs continued until the last minute, and still they were two men short. That was when old friends from Daniel's first drive to Palo Pinto showed up.

"Heard you wuz makin' a drive," Mac grinned widely. He took off his hat to wipe his head and face dry. Mac's red hair was mostly gone now, but Snake was as wiry as ever.

"Well, where did you two come from?" Daniel gave each man a hearty handshake.

"Oh, we wuz in this little scrape the North and South had, and now we're looking to take a vacation up towards Kansas and visit with the Indians a bit." He put his hat back on his head, adding, "No danger of me gettin' scalped, I reckon."

"You still hirin'?" Snake asked. "Sure could use me a job." Snake got his name because of his affinity for eating them. This made him an outsider to most, but his heart was good and loyal, and he had a charming way of playing tricks on everyone to add fun to most everything he did.

"I'm still hiring," Daniel assured him. "Couldn't have saved those last two jobs for two better men. I guess I'd be pushing my luck to find that you've been up to Abilene."

"Yes, sir, you would. But we rode a herd up to Ellsworth. It ain't as big and sin-some as Abilene yet, but they pay good money same as them."

"You men can bunk in the barn or wherever you can find a spot. After you take care of your horses, come and meet with Caleb, Coleman, and me. We need all the information we can get."

"We'll do her, Dan."

Daniel could feel his excitement growing by the hour. Also increasing was the obsession to find out everything about what might lay ahead. Since these men had been to Ellsworth, the trip could be made infinitely easier and safer. Especially if the money was the same. His head swam with possibilities and ideas. "Thank you, Lord," he breathed as he walked toward the house. "You seem to be smiling on this venture at every turn."

That night over coffee and apple pie, Daniel and Caleb made the final decision to go to Ellsworth, based on the experiences of Mac and Snake. Coleman agreed and seemed glad to have two more men who had been on a drive.

"There'd be no point in using the Goodnight Trail. It'd take us way out of our way."

Mac pointed to the map he had brought with him. "See this? We could angle up north this way, sliding east, and hit this trail. Some are beginning to call it the Western trail. Then mosey on over to the east and hit the western fork of the Chisolm. That'll take us straight into Ellsworth. 'Course it's gonna be bad riding through Indian Territory, but there ain't no other way to get there. We leaving soon, Captain?"

"Yes," said Daniel. "Are we all in agreement that this way is the trail we want to take? Coleman? Any problem?"

"No," he said carefully in front of Mary Anna, "it will be a big job no matter which way we go. Same problems. Might get us home quicker."

Mary Anna took a deep breath to steady herself. *This is what we came out here for,* she reminded herself. It was impossible not to feel their excitement, or catch some of it. They were just like little boys—only this was serious man's business.

Thaddeus came the next day. She was prepared to like the man, and she did so immediately. He was polite and seemed to fit all the requirement for which she had asked. She pointedly ignored the crutch, and he did nothing to call attention to it.

He was an enormously large bear of a man, but he was gentle spoken and took an immediate liking to the children.

"What happened to your leg, Mr. Thaddeus?" asked Betty, with a seven-year-old child's candor.

Thaddeus pulled her onto his lap and smoothed her unruly pigtails. "I lost it in the war, honey," he said calmly.

"Did it hurt?" she worried.

"For a while. Now I can use it to predict the weather. When it gets a little achy, I know it's going to rain."

"Oh, that's good. Papa'll know when to go out and plow now," she said happily. She frowned at the general laughter around her. "Well, that's important," she said, determined that the adults wouldn't get the better of her. She looked up into Thaddeus's black eyes. "If you need anything, I'll get it for you."

"Thank you very much, Betty. You're a very loving child." Thaddeus was clearly touched by her kindness.

Daniel cleared his throat. Betty took the hint, quit talking, and snuggled more deeply into Thaddeus's arms.

The last of the plans were cemented into place and Caleb and the men began saying their good evenings as they left the cabin. Daniel motioned for Thaddeus to stay behind.

"Betty, it's your bedtime." He kissed her good night and gave her a quick hug as she left. She blew a kiss to Thaddeus.

"She's a fine girl, Mr. Thornton. All your children are very well brought up."

"Thank you. The reason I asked you to stay is to tell you how relieved I am that you're going to take care of them. I'll worry only half as much on the trail," he chuckled. His face turned serious. "Once the Indians know all the men except you are gone, you're likely to be a good target for their raids."

"I know."

Daniel's serious blue eyes met Thaddeus's dependable black ones. "And you know what to do?"

"Yes, sir, I do." Thaddeus put his hand on Daniel's shoulder. "I'll take good care of your family, Daniel." He rose and left the house, his crutch making a soft clunking sound against the new wooden floor.

The next morning they were all still standing together as if posed for a portrait when Daniel nudged his horse away from them. Mary Anna was holding baby Willie, Tump had Henry on his hip, Betty was holding Thaddeus's hand, and Peter was leaning against his mother's side. Daniel could see that Mary Anna was standing her full five feet two inches. She looked like one of the children with Thaddeus in the group. Torn between the exhilaration of finally leaving on the trip and the fear of leaving his family so vulnerable, Daniel prayed silently, *God protect us all.*

Virginia and her two children stood off on the side crying. "Take good care of yourself." Caleb looked near to tears himself. He sniffed heartily into his red handkerchief. "I'll bring you and the kids a present."

Seeing Daniel leave, Caleb hurried his good-byes.

Mac was on the point, leading the herd. He and Snake would share that spot. The rest of the cowboys were strung out in pairs across the herd and riding drag. Rabbit's chuck wagon was ahead and to the left of the herd. They were already kicking up a lot of dust. Daniel's habit of wearing a clean white shirt each day would suffer on this trip. He pulled his gray Stetson down a little tighter over his forehead and rode up to the front of the herd.

The first day out would be bone tiring. The herd had to be pushed hard away from familiar range. The longhorns were cantankerous about being shoved along. They didn't seem to have a leader yet, but there were challenges being made for the spot.

Daniel kept his horse well away from the six foot spread of crooked death the longhorns carried on their heads, always mindful that one swipe at his horse could spell disaster before they even got one day out.

The two freedmen, Oliver and Maxwell, weren't thrilled at riding drag, but everyone had to take their turn at the back of the herd. The dust of a herd of any size and the constant smell of warm droppings were almost more than any man could endure for long. The next day, the two men would be rotated to another spot, much to their relief.

Daniel caught up with Mac.

"We'll stay well to the east of Twin Mountains and then trail on up the Brazos," Mac said pointing to the ragged peaks of the pale blue rock formation in the distance. "I'll scout us a camp ground for the evening." He shook his head. "If we could really push the herd, we could get to the Brazos in a few days. I'll feel better when we get through Indian territory. It's going to be too tempting for the Indians to see all these horses and cows."

"I doubt we'll be able to sneak through there, if that's what you had in mind," Daniel said wryly as he noted the huge cloud of dust the cattle made.

Mac's laugh was short.

Daniel thought of the three major rivers they had to cross before they got to Ellsworth. First the Brazos, then the Red, and finally the Canadian. *One day at a time*, he reminded himself.

A sudden rifle report threw the cattle into a wild stampede. Daniel quickly moved to the side of the herd. Looking over his should he could see a large band of Indians bearing down on them. His men began firing into the galloping raiders, and Snake rode up quickly to him.

"All we can do is try to ride the cattle down!" he shouted.

Daniel was trying to see through the dust and fire over the backs of the herd at the attacking braves. There had to be twenty men at least. *We're outnumbered,* he realized with a sinking heart. Some of the Indians had rifles, but most of them were riding low on their ponies and firing arrows from beneath their necks. Daniel dropped one young rider and eased back to help fend off the would-be rustlers. With the screams, dust, and gunshots, for one awful moment he was back in the cavalry fighting the war all over again. The fear in the pit of his stomach knotted his muscles, and he fired frantically at any target that presented itself.

The cowboys were good shots and better armed than their attackers. They stood off the determined efforts of the Indians. A few at a time, the raiders dropped away.

Daniel raced alongside the thundering herd, heading for the lead cows. Praying his horse wouldn't stumble and throw him under the deadly pounding hooves of the cattle, he tried to reach Mac.

Miles streamed by before they were able to turn the herd, crowding them together in a milling circle. It was hours more before Daniel was reasonably certain they had gathered up the cattle that had broken off from the main herd.

Mac rode up. "We did all right," he grinned. He took off his hat and wiped his balding head and the inside of his hat band. "We're closer to the Brazos River. I guess that's one way to move a herd. Not my first choice, though," he added.

"Anyone hurt?" Daniel still had a knot in his stomach.

"Nope. Rabbit's a bit shook up, cause his mules couldn't keep up with us and he was sure the Comanches wuz goin' to get him. That wagon took a beating, but he wuzn't hurt."

"He's not the only one that's shook up," Daniel said ruefully. "For a minute I thought I was back in the war."

"You are, son. You are," Mac said grimly.

"Find us a place to bed down. The men can scout for any more strays," Daniel ordered. "We've come as far as any man could hope to come the first day out."

"Yes, sir, Captain," Mac smiled slowly and rode off.

Mac's use of Daniel's title put the new war he was fighting into perspective. He was the man in charge of a group of men fighting their way to Ellsworth.

Rabbit had his promised good meal for the men that night as they camped along the edge of a small stream. Daniel had expected excited talk about their first encounter with the Indians, but the men were too tired to do much more than eat and roll up in their blankets. He sent out the night riders for guard duty and made a point to tell each man how well he had done. Then he checked to see that Rabbit had pointed the tongue of the chuck wagon to the North Star for the night. Satisfied all was well, Daniel headed for his hard bed.

Even Caleb was asleep before Daniel laid out his bedroll close to the banked fire. It had been a rough beginning, and the men had fought the raiders and the cows better than Daniel had hoped at so early a date. Now they were veterans. Surely they could handle anything.

≈

All day, Mary Anna fought loneliness. She kept waiting for Daniel to come home for supper, and then she remembered he was gone. She had been feeding so many men that the supper she prepared seemed too large, until she looked at Thaddeus. He could probably eat enough for three men.

"You're a wonderful cook, Mrs. Thornton," he complimented her as he helped himself to thirds of everything. "If you were cooking at the boarding house, we'd have a lot more business."

She smiled her thanks, remembering the times she had already spent at that job back in East Texas where her father owned a hotel. Her face took on a dreamy look as she remembered Daniel staying there and how she had fed him supper in the dining room, and how they had fallen in love and married. East Texas seemed years away. The last time she had been there was during the war when Daniel had been away fighting.

The only pleasant memory from those difficult war years was the face of the Reverend Amos Strong. Amos, the man whose friendship had sustained her through those bad years. *I wonder where he is and how he is? And if he ever married. He was so kind to me and my children.*

"Happy memories?" Thaddeus asked.

Mary Anna laughed. "Some. I used to cook in my father's hotel a long time ago. You triggered some memories."

She shook off yesterday and lived through the chores of today. The small herd of choice cattle Daniel had left for breeding as well as the horses Mary Anna would need were all penned in the small corral closest to the house. It would be easy to hear anyone who might come in the night to steal. She also had the two dogs. Surely they were ready.

"I'll check with Mrs. West to see if she needs anything," Thaddeus said.

Mary Anna's final precaution was to retrieve the lovely new rifle Daniel had left for her and prop it right beside her as she crawled into the empty bed, praying that nothing would disturb their sleep.

Much to Mary Anna's surprise, the night passed uneventfully. The day was so beautiful she decided to make soap. She looked around for her two older boys, but apparently they had anticipated the giant job she had in mind and had disappeared. One thing Mary Anna insisted on was that everyone learn to do everything. The excuse, "That's girls' work," only made her more determined that her children would be totally independent when they went out on their own.

She had Betty watch the baby and Thaddeus carry out the huge black kettle and lay the fire. She shouted for Virginia to come out and help her.

"You make the soap, and I'll do the wash," Virginia said. Either job was a backbreaking one, but with the two of them to talk and laugh, both tasks went faster.

Mary Anna and Virginia spread out the clean wash on the rope Daniel had strung out between two poles. But with so many articles of clothing, they used the bushes and anything else they could to let the hot sun dry them.

Almost, Mary Anna forgot to be alert for signs of raiders. But in the lull of the midafternoon, a raiding party of about ten men came swooping in, firing bullets and arrows.

"Run for the house!" Mary Anna yelled at the older children. While she grabbed the baby, Virginia and Thaddeus grabbed the younger children and everyone dashed for cover. As soon as they had the door shut and bolted, Mary Anna grabbed her new rifle and fired through the shutters that the older boys had partially closed. Virginia and Thaddeus covered the other two walls. Tump was manfully watching through the back window and firing at every brave he saw.

But it was impossible to see what was happening to the stock behind the corral. Mary Anna had the sinking feeling they were about to be left without a single animal.

The four fired relentlessly until they drove the men away. It was only then that they could check the stock.

Thunder, Tump's beloved horse, was missing.

"They got him again!" wailed Tump.

Mary Anna tried to comfort him. "Maybe he'll get loose again like he did last time. He knows his way home."

Angry as she was at the theft, she almost sat down and cried when she saw what had happened to all the washing she and Virginia had so carefully done. Some of it had been knocked off the bushes and stomped by careless hooves, and the rest was covered with dust. When she started picking up the scattered laundry, she discovered it had been shot through with bullets. She stood there, the bright sun glinting off the red in her auburn hair, and literally bit her tongue to keep from saying the things she was thinking.

The sorrow that for years she had felt for the Indians was rapidly evaporating under the constant attacks on her home and possessions. She sighed. There was nothing to do but wash everything again and try to mend the holes.

As she and Virginia redid the wash together, reality set in. "What are we going to do now?" Virginia asked.

"I don't know. We have Thaddeus and plenty of fire power, but we don't have any horses or any other way of getting word out about our situation. I guess we hold out until someone comes to us." She looked at Virginia's pale face. "You might as well move in with us. I'll feel safer," she said to keep her friend from having to ask. "We can hold out a long time. Don't worry, the Lord will take care of this, too. Lieutenant Mooreland is supposed to bring us the money for the horses. He'll be back soon," she said confidently.

Mary Anna's body ached from bending over the wash kettles, and she leaned back with her hand on her side to stretch. The rapidly growing child inside of her gave a protesting kick. "I'm tired, too," she said to the unborn child. She looked at all the newly washed laundry and got mad all over again.

That night she angrily poked the needle into every stitch she made as she repaired the garments by lamplight.

three

Mac moved the herd away from the Brazos and headed toward the Red River. There had been no more attempts to steal the cattle, but Daniel knew there were too many miles left to hope it wouldn't happen again.

At the noon break Daniel and Coleman were leaning against the wheels of the chuck wagon. It was hot and muggy, but the sky was a peaceful blue.

"It hasn't been too bad yet," Daniel said between bites of Rabbit's wonderful food.

"Only one stampede and raid," Coleman grinned. His voice sobered. "You know it ain't over yet."

"I know. I can understand the Indian men not wanting to stay on the reservation. It really hems them in. That's one of the reasons I came out here, feeling hemmed in."

"But them stealing from you does nothing to endear them to your heart," Coleman smiled. "You know, we took everything from them. How's a young buck supposed to prove he can provide for a family? Or be brave in battle? That's their way of life, and they can't do that on the reservation."

"With the buffalo gone, they have to use our herd, huh?" Daniel sopped his biscuit in his bean juice. "But the government gives them meat. They have an agent for that."

Coleman's eyes glinted in anger. "Most of those agents are thieves. And the meat the Indians do get—if they get it—is spoiled."

"It's too big a problem for me to solve," said Daniel shaking his head helplessly. "I came out here to make a living for me and my family. I had no intentions of ruining anyone's life." He stood up and threw the remains of his coffee on the ground. "Let's move 'em out."

But the pleasure of seeing his and Caleb's cattle moving to market was tainted. He wanted a glorious adventure, but not at the cost of people's lives. His motives were pure and simple. He wanted to have a ranch. He needed to move his cattle. That should be all there was to it. He tried to put the rest of the problem out of his mind. He focused his thoughts on Mary Anna, waiting at home.

Her absence was like a living thing within him. Half of him was at the ranch and half of him was here. It still amazed him that his love for one woman could have remained so strong through all these years. It had grown from the first desires of the young to the deep need of being together, touching—of knowing someone so well that words weren't needed between them. He loved his children, but they were an extension of his and Mary Anna's love for each other. He loved Mary Anna, and he smiled broadly as he remembered that he was the only man she loved.

The heavy still air around him made Daniel perspire heavily, and the dust from the cattle stuck to him from top to bottom. The heavy leather chaps he wore to protect his legs from the tearing fingers of the brush they were moving through caught the sun and made his denim pants damp. Worse yet, he knew this was exactly the kind of weather that could change in moments to a bad storm.

He scanned the horizon but saw only a few cumulus clouds floating like fully bloomed out cotton bolls. Though they were fair weather clouds and nothing to be alarmed at, he didn't drop his guard. Things in Texas could move very quickly and be deadly for the man who failed to stay alert.

His sorrel gelding stepped lightly over the rocky terrain. He was surefooted and a comfort to Daniel, who knew he wouldn't have to guide the horse around obstacles like some horses he had ridden. He and Rusty had been together for two years. They knew each other well, moving as one over country that was sometimes the same color as the horse. Daniel paid attention to Rusty's moods. He knew the horse possessed keener senses than he did. If Rusty was restless, Daniel became alert to everything around him, anticipating a problem of some kind. He disliked the days he had to let Rusty rest in the remuda and ride another horse. Those days never seemed to go as well.

That night they bedded the cattle down beside a large spring that fed a small lake. It was still hot at sundown.

"I waited for the sun to go down and those good old Texas breezes to spring up and blow this wet away," complained Mac as he spread his blankets close to Daniel's. He let go of the saddle he was carrying, arranged it at the top of his blankets for his pillow, and dropped down on the lumpy earthen bed.

Daniel sighed audibly. "You aren't going to get much sleep tonight, Mac. The mosquitoes are eating me alive over here."

Mac smiled angelically. "I've never had me a mosquito bite in my life," he bragged. "They don't seem to cotton to me."

"Maybe it's your smell," Coleman shot back from his place nearby.

"Maybe," Mac grinned good-naturedly. "I plan to take me a bath tomorrow, if I have time. That little lake looks mighty invitin'."

"Be careful of the reeds," Coleman said casually. "That's usually where the water moccasins are hiding."

Had the moon been brighter, both men would have seen Mac pale in its glow. But he said in a strong voice. "I'll wear my hat and keep my gun in it." Then with a gleam in his eye, he added, "I noticed you hang your boots up on a tree limb. What's that for?" he asked Coleman.

"Keeps the scorpions and snakes out of them, airs them out, and keeps away rheumatism," he said confidently.

Daniel listened to the bantering and joined in. "Did you notice that Maxwell always puts his rope in a circle around his bed?" He paused dramatically. "Says a rattlesnake won't cross over a rope. His mammy down on the plantation told him that."

"Does that work?" asked Coleman doubtfully.

"He hasn't been bitten yet," Daniel said with a poker face.

"Hmm," said Coleman, "it's something to consider."

"I doubt I'll get half a night's sleep worrying about if a snake is going to crawl in my bed tonight without my rope," said Mac in a half-serious tone. Then he grinned widely in the night. He knew Coleman would get less than a full night's sleep, worrying about whether snakes were going to slither into his unprotected bed.

The soothing sounds of the night rider's song to the cattle calmed Daniel, and after a full day in the saddle, he slept soundly despite his dislike of sleeping on the ground.

At dawn he was awakened by the aroma of strong coffee boiling over a clean hot fire and the smell of biscuits baking in the big covered pan Rabbit had resting in the coals around the edge of the fire.

He rolled out, stretched to get the kinks out, and pulled on his boots. Mac's bedroll was put away, and when Daniel squinted into the eastern sun at the small lake, he could see Mac's hat bobbing up and down as he enjoyed the water.

"Rise and shine, Coleman. It's time for our baths and rinsing out a few things." He nudged Coleman's foot with the toe of his boot.

Coleman slid his hat off his face and took a deep breath. "Not without my coffee first." The two men took their tin cups with them to the lake.

They stripped down to their long johns, and Coleman stretched out at the edge of the water, drinking his coffee. "Now this is what I call heavenly."

Daniel finished off his coffee and waded out to Mac.

"Here, hold my hat while I get under the water for a few minutes. I've got mud in my hair from the trail."

The water felt deliciously cool in the early morning, for the high humidity had not gone away in the night. Their baths wouldn't last longer than their first few minutes on the trail, but they felt wonderful for the moment.

Daniel saw Caleb squatted down at the edge of the water talking to Coleman. "Come on in, Caleb," he shouted. "It feels grand!"

Caleb shouted back. "No, thanks, I don't want to catch my death on the first part of the trip. I'll wait until we have to ride across a river. Too much bathing is bad for the body."

Rabbit rang the big triangle with his cooking spoon to call in the outlying cowboys. The smell alone was enough to have most of the men up and moving around, waiting to be called.

While they ate their breakfast, Daniel and Caleb talked.

"I don't like this weather, Dan," Caleb said. "I 'spect we're in for some big thunder-boomers before long."

"Yeah, I think you're right. All we can do is watch and hope we can find some kind of shelter when it hits."

After the weeks they had been on the trail, the drive was

taking on a certain monotony. "Herding is a lot like the War," Caleb remarked. "Either it's boring or gut tearing."

"I like the boring part," Daniel smiled.

They were nearing the Red River. The small settlement of Doans was nearby, and Daniel thought he might ride over and pick up a few supplies, but a cloud was building in the west and he didn't like the looks of it. A towering thunderhead was rapidly getting larger and taller. Its top was flattening out, a sure sign of a storm cloud. The slight green cast to it suggested hail, and the day was even more oppressively humid. They were miles from any shelter, and Daniel knew they could be in for a bad time. He spoke to Mac. "Do you know a place we could hole up?"

Mac surveyed the sky. "Nothing but a small ravine over towards the west a few miles."

"Better head the herd over that way. We could be in for some real bad weather."

By noontime camp, the wind had picked up and was blowing things around. Rabbit secured the canvas tarp more tightly over the supplies. The men broke out their ponchos and prepared for a dunking. The cattle were edgy and kept breaking away from the main herd. The darkening sky looked uglier as the afternoon moved on.

A single rumble of thunder like a low growl crawled across the herd, causing some of the cows to bolt. The men were hard-pressed to keep the herd together. They moved them down into the ravine and circled them continuously, trying to calm them.

Daniel saw small balls of lightening jump from horn to horn on the cows near him. He knew about ball lightening, or St. Elmo's fire, as the cowboys called it, but it was unnerving to see the brightly glowing balls jump between the horns of the cattle or roll along the ground. It made the cows dodge about, and the sound of their long, crooked horns clicked loudly like a hundred demented swordsmen dueling on the endless prairie.

When the hail started, it was pea-sized, but rapidly grew to the size of small plums.

Daniel heard the rumbling of the cattle as they began trying to move away from the pelting balls of ice. The noise was unusually loud. The rumbling was growing out of proportion to the number of cattle. It was then he saw that part of the cloud had dropped down in an evil-looking black tail. It was sucking up dirt and grass as it traveled. It looked to be about a quarter of a mile away, and it was coming right at them.

"Cyclone!" screamed Mac as he raced toward Daniel. "Get off your horse and lay flat!"

"But the cattle!" Daniel shouted back.

"Never mind them. Take care of yourself!"

It was black as night, and the horrible rumbling was growing into a grinding scream as it came closer. Daniel tried to get his horse to lie down, but the animal's eyes were wild with fright and he fought to get free. A bolt of lightning struck nearby, sending Rusty rearing into the air, pawing and screaming. Daniel felt the reins being ripped from his hands, so he jammed his Stetson tighter on his head and pressed his face closer to the earth. Water from the deluge splashed up into his face as he flattened himself as close to the earth as he could get. The roar was deafening. He thought he'd already seen the worst nature could hurl at him, but past tussles paled in comparison to this cyclone.

The roaring seemed to last forever, but even as the banshee din moved away from them, the rain continued. Great slashing curtains threatened to wash them all away. Daniel struggled to his feet. He was disoriented. In the waves of rain he couldn't distinguish the herd or hear any of the other cowboys. He stood still, trying to get his bearings, when someone rode up behind him.

"You all right, Captain?" shouted Snake over the rain.

"Lost my horse," he shouted back. Snake offered him a hand up, and he climbed on behind the drenched man. The mare didn't like the noise and she didn't like the two riders, so she promptly tried to throw them both off her back. They held their seats and steadied her.

A little farther along, they found the chuck wagon. The tornado-force winds had toppled it, and Rabbit was crouched beneath.

"Are you hurt, Rabbit?" Daniel called.

"Naw, sir, jest scairt to death." His eyes were big under his rain-soaked hat.

"Stay here until we find the herd. We'll come back and help right the wagon for you."

"This mother's child ain't goin' nowheres, you can bet your hat on that!" shouted Rabbit.

The rain begin to let up a little, and they spotted the herd. The other men had already begun rounding up the scattered cows. To Daniel's great delight, Oliver, the other freedman, came up leading Rusty.

They made a very wet camp that night. There wasn't a piece of dry wood to be had, so the men wrapped up as well as they could against the drizzle and chose high ground to set up the small tents they carried.

Mac was heard to grumble as he worked on the tent, "And I wasted a perfectly good bath just to get rained on."

Caleb chuckled. "I told you to wait." He climbed into the

tent with Daniel. "I'd almost rather fight Indians as to sit out in the night in the rain. Even if it is in a tent." Water was running off his hat from the small hole in the canvas.

"Just try to think of all that money," replied Daniel as he ran an ineffective hand across his face to wipe away the water. His fingers rubbed the new growth of beard he'd acquired since he'd left home. Rarely did any of the men spend time shaving on a drive. Of course, some of them were so young, it didn't matter.

"That beard makes you look nearly as old as me," Caleb remarked.

"It stays until just before we get back home," Daniel said firmly.

Caleb grinned. "Mary Anna wouldn't recognize her slicked up husband now. No clean white shirt, no shaving, sleeping on the ground."

Daniel took his kidding well. "The only reason I got all slicked up was so I could catch a woman like Mary Anna. Now I got her, but she can't see me. And I'll bet she'll love a slicked up rich cattle baron even better."

The morning brought the soggy sun. A clear path showed where the raging funnel had ripped its way across the landscape. Grass, bushes, and a few cows lay sprawled like broken toys. Awe, fear, and relief passed in stages across each man's face as they looked at the evidence of the powerful storm.

"Thank You, Lord, that we lived to finish this drive," breathed Daniel.

"Amen," added Rabbit.

A sobered group of men rounded up the scattered herd. Soon the whistles and shouts of the cowboys urging the cattle along was heard again. This time they weren't battling the dust. It was the mud and other obstacles left by the storm that could have killed them all.

When they reached the Red River, the men were in no mood to get wet again so soon. The last miles to the river had been hard ones, so Daniel ordered a camp on its banks. They would ford it in the morning. He was not surprised to find the river flooded after the recent rain. The sand around the river was treacherous, and the Red had a reputation for dangerous quicksand and slow death.

"Where did you cross before?" Daniel asked Mac.

"Don't matter where we went before, the quicksand changes every day. There's a trading post on down the river. Man that owns it has a squaw that knows the ways of the river. 'Course he'll charge us, but she'll find a safe way over."

The next morning when Mac came back, a squaw rode a pinto behind him. Serenely Kititke, or Precious One, used a long pole and poked out the safe passage for the men and cattle, her money already tucked inside her bright red blouse.

The place she chose was free of quicksand, but the mud and current were hard on horses and cattle alike. It got worse with each churning hoof that stirred it. Daniel went back and forth, pushing the reluctant cows into the swirling water. The current was swift, and he had to post men downstream to block the drifting cattle. Before he had ridden to the other side of the herd, Daniel's saddle blanket was soaked and Rusty was visibly tiring.

On the far side, Daniel got off Rusty and helped the men pulling Rabbit and his chuck wagon across with ropes. Rabbit's hands clenched the reins, looking like claws. But Savannah was surefooted and gave confidence to her partner, Alabama, so they made it across the Red River in good shape.

Rabbit got down and rubbed the mules' noses. "You sure done good, honey. You sure done good."

"The next one won't be so hard, Rabbit," promised Snake.

"Oh, no! The next one! I needs to get over this one before we talk about another one."

Maxwell rode up. "Stop actin' like a sissy schoolgirl. You're a real cowboy. This here is your third drive. You been through most everythin' already. Now, stand up and get them mules moving. Don't make me ashamed of you." He sat proudly in the saddle, and though he was the same age as Rabbit, he looked years older and years more confident. "Move," he ordered again and rode off to help with the herd.

Rabbit was mumbling to himself as he checked over his chuck wagon for damage. But he stood up taller as Maxwell had told him.

❧

Mary Anna and Virginia were feeding cornbread and cold buttermilk for lunch to their combined families, when Tump held his piece of cornbread in midair, his mouth open slightly, and stared through the open door.

"What's wrong, Tump?" asked Mary Anna in alarm.

He didn't answer—instead knocking his chair over as he bolted from the house. When Mary Anna stood in the door, she could see the reason for Tump's strange behavior.

"Well, I'll be double dipped in chocolate," she said. Thaddeus looked over her shoulder. There was pandemonium as they all tumbled out of the cabin for a look.

"Thunder!" said Mary Anna. "Thank You, Jesus," she breathed as she ran out to watch Tump throw his arms around the horse's neck and run unbelieving hands across his nose.

"Look at that. Another broken buckskin rope. Thunder, you're getting a reputation among those Indians," breathed

Mary Anna. "Well, quit petting him, Tump, and take him to the barn and feed and water him. He looks all right to me." She turned questioningly to Thaddeus.

"Looks good to me, too. He hasn't been mistreated. That's got to be the smartest horse I've ever seen to get away from the Indians twice."

"Well, they won't get him again, I can promise you that," Tump said flatly. "I'm going to sleep with him all the time now." The excited voices of the children almost drowned out his statement.

But mothers have good ears, and Mary Anna said, "No, you're not, but we'll think of something."

While Tump led the procession to the barn, Thaddeus said, "I'll sleep out here, if you like."

Her reply was immediate. "No, I want you at the house with us." She smiled grimly. "Who knows? They may decide no horse is going to escape from them again and come for him just to make a point."

"But he is our only horse," argued Virginia.

Mary Anna thought for a moment. "We'll move Thaddeus into the house and put Thunder in the shed by the house. Sorry, Thaddeus, but you'll have to take out that floor."

"I can do it in the wink of an eye," he promised. "Everything is going to be just fine."

But Thaddeus didn't see the shadow that blended itself into the trees at the edge of the woods. The eyes were mocking. Taking back the horse he had chosen for himself was child's play. This time he had an uglier plan. It was time for these interlopers to be swept from his land. The dappled sunlight barely revealed the copper-colored face and the distinctive triple-braided hair tied with fur, two feathers rakishly stuck in the braids framing his face.

As he strode toward his horse, the face of Santana was grim. His heart still felt like a burning hot stone in his chest. These settlers had taken his wife and child from him. His dry eyes could not let go of the picture of his family as he had found them—dead. The white settlers must pay for taking away everything that was dear to him. His family, his way of life. He slid on his horse and glided away, still a shadow on the hill.

There was a bit of shuffling to do to accommodate all the people in the cabin that night, but Mary Anna knew it was prudent for them to be together. Even Thaddeus's snore from in front of the fireplace was comforting.

The scorching Texas days were giving way to cooler nights now that it was fall. Mary Anna thought of Daniel on the trail, and wondered if he had reached Ellsworth yet. She prayed for him and his men, and then she prayed for her "family" in the cabin.

ਰ

The next week she was startled to see two Indians riding calmly up the road toward the cabin. They carried no drawn weapons, and she stood at the front of the door with her hand on the rifle as Thaddeus met them. He had his rifle in his free hand as he hobbled out.

After a few minutes of conversation, he came back to Mary Anna. The men sat impassively on their horses, watching him.

"They want tobacco and meat. They said they know only a one-legged man guards the cabin."

"So, we're back to blackmail again," she said angrily.

"I told them because I have only one leg, I have two hearts for courage. And a woman who has the heart of a panther."

She smiled. "And. . . ," she coached.

"And they said since we were so brave, they were sure we could spare some extra meat." Thaddeus's forehead shone with perspiration. "What do you want to do?"

Mary Anna honestly didn't know. The Indians were not starved or poorly clad. One of the men had his hair parted down the middle, then each side had been braided into three braids, ending in a single point tied with fur. Two feathers had been stuck in at a rakish angle and framed his face. The other man was wearing a tall stovepipe hat, much like the one she had seen the minister in Tennessee Colony wear. It made a shudder ripple through her small frame to think of where he might have gotten it.

From the corner of her eye, Mary Anna saw a horse move by the corral. One of the Indians pulled a gun. Thaddeus shoved her roughly into the cabin, slamming the heavy door behind them. Immediately a deep thud was heard against it.

"Close the shutters!" she screamed at Tump. He sprinted for them and got his rifle. They worked together as before. Jim, Virginia's oldest boy, lifted the hinged door on the cellar and led the terrified children down to safety.

"Mama!" screamed Tump. "They're trying to get Thunder out of the shed!" The big horse was shying away from the brave, fighting frantically at the rope that been thrown around his neck.

"Not this time," Tump said as he shot at the brave, who fell gracefully from his horse. But Tump uttered a single moan of anguish as another Indian took deliberate aim and shot an arrow deep into the horse's neck. "No, no, no," Tump kept saying as he shot at the Indians.

Mary Anna expected the raiders to leave once they had shot Thunder, but they continued with a ferocity that deeply frightened her. *It isn't just the horse they want. They want to drive us out. They want to kill us.*

Arrows and bullets were thundering into the heavy sides of the cabin. With the shutters closed, the Indians had few targets at which to shoot. They surrounded the cabin and pelted all four walls with continuous fire until they finally made a retreat, taking their dead and wounded with them.

Tump sprinted for the door, straining as he lifted the heavy log that barred it.

"No, Tump!" shouted Mary Anna, and she pushed him away from the door.

"But Thunder may still be alive!" he sobbed.

"We can't go out there yet." Thaddeus's voice was firm. He went to all the windows, peeking through the gun slits. It looked safe enough, but he knew it could be a ruse to get them outside.

They waited a full thirty minutes before venturing out. Thaddeus and Tump walked cautiously and fully armed to the fallen animal.

Tump flung himself down on Thunder. The horse whinnied pitifully. An arrow buried deeply in his neck, and blood ran into his beautiful mane. Tump didn't try to stem the tears washing down his face. "Can't we take it out?" he cried to Thaddeus. "Mama's a good doctor. She can save him."

Thaddeus saw no blood coming from the horse's mouth. That was a good sign, even though the animal had lost a lot of blood from the wound. He stood up and motioned for Mary Anna to come.

"Oh, Tump," was all she said when she saw Thunder.

"You can make him well, Mama. You saved Pap when he got shot with an arrow at the plum thicket."

Mary Anna and Thaddeus exchanged glances. "He's lost a lot of blood, son." But when she saw the pitiful sadness of her child, she had no choice but to try.

"See if you can get him on his feet. We need to get him to the shed before I try to take out the arrow."

Thunder struggled to his knees and finally to his feet. Mary Anna was amazed at his strength. Gently they walked him to the shed, and he lay down on the straw with a deep sigh.

"Fetch me the skinning knife," she ordered. She tried to do all the things she had done for Daniel. Fortunately, the arrow had passed through the animal's slender neck. She cut off the arrowhead and carefully retracted the shaft. Thunder sensed she was trying to help him and lay quietly under her hands.

She cleaned the wound with witch hazel and made a poultice of healing herbs, holding it in place with long pieces of torn cloth that she wrapped around Thunder's neck. "That's all I can do. It's up to Thunder and the Lord now."

She let Tump sleep in the little shed, with Thaddeus on guard. But it wasn't Thunder she was remembering that night as she lay in bed. It was the black eyes of the two warriors who had demanded the meat. They were not afraid of being at the cabin. There had been neither animosity nor friendship in their faces. Their expressions had been unreadable. Mary Anna cringed in the dark at the memory and prayed earnestly for protection.

When morning came, she fully expected to find a weeping Tump. Once inside the shed she was surprised to find the horse in bad shape, but still alive. She changed the poultice and was relieved to see that the bleeding had pretty much stopped and that there were no signs of festering.

"You are a good doctor," Thaddeus saluted her. She tried not to smile at the compliment

"Let's not get too happy yet. It will be a while before we know for sure if Thunder will live." Even if he did, they were still without a horse for the moment.

Thaddeus read her thoughts. "Someone will come," he said quietly. "We'll be fine until they do."

Mary Anna continued to pray for deliverance, and when it came, she was surprised by the source. Lieutenant Mooreland and a small company of men rode up to the cabin to deliver payment for the ten horses.

"I'm so glad to see you," Mary Anna greeted the young man. "We've been raided, and all we have is one injured horse. Could you ride back into Stephenville and have Charlie send us a horse or two? I can pay him."

"No one was hurt in the raid?" he asked gallantly. Mary Anna was very pleasing to the eye, and her manner was polished.

"My husband has built us a strong fortress. We can defend ourselves, I believe. But we must have a horse." She noted the dusty uniforms of the men. "Have your men feed and water their horses, and I'll feed you all some lunch." She shaded her face with her hand as looked up into Lieutenant Mooreland's face. He gave a friendly smile and dismounted.

Sitting at the table with the rest of the "family" while his men lounged in the shade enjoying a hearty meal, the lieutenant said, "You can be sure we'll get by here as often as we can. We're spread very thin, but knowing you're here with only one man on the place makes you a priority. How long will your husbands be gone?"

"We hope they'll be back before December," Virginia answered.

Thaddeus was silently watching the lieutenant. He had his doubts about anyone representing Union forces, but it would make things safer if the lieutenant and his men came around more often. Maybe the Indians would stay away when they noticed the military presence.

four

Daniel felt as if he had been away from home a lifetime. They had successfully forded the Red River and were headed for the Canadian. He used the rivers to mentally count off the stages of the trip.

They had made better time than he had hoped so far. At the rate they were going, he might be home by December—provided there weren't any major problems.

Caleb rode up beside him as they scouted ahead of the herd. "You know, Dan, we've been mighty lucky on this drive."

"Not lucky, Caleb," he corrected, "blessed."

"Yeah, you're right. Anyhow, there haven't been more raids. We've lost a few cows in the night, but we're in the middle of Indian country, so what can you expect? I don't mind feeding a few families."

"Did you double the night guard? I do mind feeding more than we have to."

"Yup. I saw Maxwell sleeping in the saddle on the way up here to you." He took off his neckerchief and wiped his perspiring face. "The nights are getting colder, but it sure do get hot during the day, don't it?"

Daniel nodded. His eyes scanned the horizon constantly, looking for trouble.

"Aren't we cutting back a little to the west?" Caleb asked.

"Yes. Mac heard about a farmer that doesn't cotton to trail drives, so we're skirting his land to avoid any trouble."

"I'm not sure it worked. Here come three riders, and they ain't riding like cowboys."

Daniel and Caleb kept riding, and as the three men drew nearer, they could see them more clearly. "Looks like a man and his two boys," Caleb said.

"They don't look like boys to me," Daniel said through gritted teeth. "Look at all the artillery they're carrying. They're better armed than we were at the end of the war." He slid his rifle out of its holster beside his leg on the saddle and positioned it across his lap. Caleb did the same, only he took out a shotgun, which would do much more damage at close range.

The riders stopped a talking distance away. Without preamble the man said in a nasty voice, "This here is my land. Don't want no cattle spoiling it. Name's Hippleworth and these here are my boys."

"We don't want any trouble," said Daniel in a friendly manner. "Where are the boundaries of your land? We'd be glad to go 'round it."

"Cain't lessen you aim to go into the next territory."

"You own and work that much land?" Daniel asked carefully.

The old man's eyes were crafty. "Between you herders churning up the land and the Indians, I can hardly make a living. Might make a bargain, though," he added as though he had just though of a plan.

"We're listening and reasonable."

"You could pay me for crossing over my land. Say about a dollar a head. That seems reasonable to me and my boys." The two ugly men with him grinned evilly and shook their heads in agreement.

Caleb and Daniel exchanged surprised looks. It was clearly

highway robbery, and everyone sitting there knew it.

"Would you settle for fifty cents?" Daniel countered.

The old man's eyes glittered as he surveyed the herd stretched out for miles behind the men. "Seventy-five," he said.

"Sixty and not a cent more," Daniel pressed.

"Only if you let me and the boys count the cows." The old man had them, and he knew it. Daniel couldn't go around what the old man claimed was his, and he didn't want to risk a gunfight.

"My foreman will be glad to help you with the counting," Daniel added. He was getting perilously low on hard cash. He wondered if there were any other "farmers" waiting between him and Ellsworth.

While the men counted the cattle, he also wondered if he'd ever get home again. If he wasn't helping Mac find water, they were fording unfriendly rivers that tried to suck his cows under. There was always the threat of Indians, rustlers, and rattlesnakes. Storms lurked in every heavy cloud. About the only thing they hadn't encountered was a prairie fire. He figured that was simply waiting for them around the corner.

That night, they camped for the evening well past the "farm" of Mr. Hippleworth and his boys. Of course, the man's count had been higher than Mac's, so they agreed to split the difference. "To keep peace in the family," Mac had grinned falsely.

Even though it had been weeks since the storm, the men talked endlessly about it as they sat around the campfire after supper. Most of them had never seen a storm of that magnitude. Snake said he had seen plenty.

"I've seen 'em pick up a whole barn and put it down a

mile away. Or just blow it to smithereens, like four cannons had fired on it at once."

One of the men eased out a low, long whistle.

"I seen a chicken that had been picked up, and then set back down," Snake continued. "The chicken was fine, but every feather on her was plumb gone offen that hen."

"Ah, go on, Snake. That sounds like some of them tall Texas tales," Toad said.

"Naw, it's truth. I've even seen people picked up. Some wuz fine, and some had ever bone in their body broke."

Silence greet that last statement, for most of them had thought that could certainly have happened to them, given the strength of the storm they had endured.

"Worse part is, that this is the time of year that they happen most. It could happen again," Snake added with a sad-looking face.

Before Snake could completely spook the men, Mac called for the night riders, and Maxwell pulled out his harmonica and began a cheerful tune, easing the tension of the camp.

Caleb came up to Daniel. "Sure am glad we have that happy soul to cheer us up when things go bad."

"I'm afraid some of what he says is too true to be ignored, but I'll be dipped in lye water if I know what to do about it." Daniel turned his back to the men for more privacy. "Tell you what, Caleb, the Lord is testing my faith on a daily basis."

"You ought ter be getting big spiritual muscles," Caleb smiled. "We're getting close now. Another two weeks. You and the Lord can surely work out something for that time, cain't ya?"

"Caleb, I'll swan if you aren't starting to sound just like Mary Anna. That's all I need," Daniel grumbled, "a trail wife." But he knew Caleb was right, and he prayed longer that night before he fell asleep.

The next morning Caleb noted his friend looked more rested. "We've made good time," he said affably.

Daniel laughed. "Between the Indians stampeding us and the cyclone blowing the entire herd thirty miles up the trail, we've done well. By the time we get home, that storm story will have us flying the last leg of the trip."

Caleb joined his laughter. "Wished it wuz that easy, Dan."

❧

Things had eased up some for Mary Anna. True to his word, Lieutenant Mooreland had gone into town, and Charlie, the storekeeper, had sent a man out with a horse for them.

Thunder was walking on wobbly legs, but he had gained his feet again. Mary Anna insisted Tump and Thaddeus sleep in the house again. She was still worried the Indians would come again on the Comanche moon that would soon be rising. Thaddeus, Tump, and Jim enlarged the shed so that both horses could be stabled next to the cabin.

"The Comanche moon will rise in the next few days," Virginia said softly as they cooked supper.

"We'll be ready, Virginia. I've felt such peace today. I feel that Daniel is safe, even though I haven't heard from him."

"It reminds you of the war, doesn't it?"

"Yes." Mary Anna wandered back to that time in her mind and whispered, "I never got a letter from him the whole time he was gone. Two years." She came back to the business of preparing the meal. "But I never gave up hope that he was alive. Amos Strong helped me through that time. You remember me telling you about Reverend Strong, don't you?"

"Yes." Virginia's eyes danced with mischief. "Did you ever tell Daniel that Reverend Strong was in love with you?"

Mary Anna tried to look indignant. "He was not in love with me. Not exactly. And anyway, he was always a complete gentleman. I have nothing to be ashamed of in my friendship with Amos."

"I know. But did you ever tell Daniel?" she insisted.

Mary Anna's gaze went down. "No, but I'm sure he knew after he met Amos. He was wonderful about it, Virginia. He never thought the worst. Never accused me of being unfaithful to him. In fact, he became good friends with Amos himself."

"Daniel is one in a million, I got to admit." She couldn't help asking, "Do you ever think of him? Amos, I mean."

"Sometimes when I bake an apple cobbler. He loved apple cobbler." She shook her head in dismay. "We were talking about Daniel. I don't want to go back to the past. Not even one day. Daniel is well and happy and safe. I'm sure of that. And he could be home in a month or less." Her eyes sparkled like deep blue sapphires with anticipation.

Mary Anna, Thaddeus, and Virginia slept very lightly during the Comanche moon, but there wasn't a raid. A few days later, they learned that the Indians had attacked another homestead.

That night, Mary Anna was awakened by Henry and Willie coughing. Terror gripped her heart. She had heard that sound too often before. As she feared, when she checked on the younger boys, both of them had scarlet circles on their little dry cheeks. Instantly she woke up the other adults.

"Thaddeus, take the other children over to the Wests' cabin and keep them there," Mary Anna ordered. "I don't want them sick too."

Virginia mad a soothing willow tea for the fever, and Mary Anna bathed the boys' foreheads with cool water. They coughed until their tiny bodies were almost too weak to cough again.

She tried every remedy that she and Virginia could think of and spooned hearty soup down their little throats. Sometimes they couldn't get the liquid down because they were coughing so hard. Days passed with no change. The nights were the worst. The little boys would cough until they lost their breath. Mary Anna and Virginia took turns pressing on the children's chests to make them breathe in, and they propped the boys high on pillows to ease their labored breaths. Their eyes were bright with fever, but they didn't have enough energy to cry. Mary Anna constantly prayed that the boys would be healed as she tried all her powders and potions on them.

In the Wests' cabin Betty clung close to Thaddeus, who was feeling the fear that a helpless man feels when children are dangerously ill. She climbed into his lap, wrapped her arms around his thick neck and asked, "Will they die?"

"We're all praying that they won't, but they're awful sick."

"I've never seen anyone dead," she said thoughtfully.

"I thank God for that," he said as he remembered the carnage of the war. "Dying is not bad for the people that go. They get to live in heaven, and nothing goes wrong up there."

Sagely she asked, "Then why is Mama so worried about them going to such a wonderful place?"

"She needs them down here with her. She loves them and would miss them if they went away forever." Thaddeus stroked her long pigtails with gentle fingers.

"Like she's missing Papa, I guess." Thaddeus smiled and nodded. "But Papa's coming back, isn't he? Mama said soon."

"Yes, he'll be back." Thaddeus hoped to heaven he wasn't lying.

"Peter says I have another brother and two sisters, but they died and went to heaven."

Wistfully Betty added, "I would like to have those sisters. I like to play dolls, and the boys won't play with me very much." She whispered to him, "I think that last baby Papa buried a long time ago was a girl. Sometimes I go there and talk to her. I heard Mama call her Snow once when I went down there with her to put flowers on the grave. So I call her Snow, too. It's a pretty name. Mama said that's how long the baby lived. Like the spring snow. I don't remember it." She sighed. "Snow is a pretty name, not like Betty." Her freckled face was solemn.

"I love your name. *Elizabeth* means 'consecrated to God.'"

"But my name is *Betty*," she argued.

"That's your love name. Elizabeth is your real name. Betty means the same thing," he assured her. "It means you're special to Him."

She took in a long breath. "I'm special to God." She turned her light gray eyes up to him. "Mama says God loves all of us, and watches over us. He'll take care of Henry and Willie, too. They'll be all right. Even if they die," she added confidently.

Thaddeus choked back the flood of tears forming in his eyes. "Yes, little Elizabeth, they'll be all right."

After days of numbing fatigue for all the adults, the boys' fever broke and the coughing eased. Mary Anna came to get the other children after she was sure the boys were on the road to recovery. Thaddeus told her of his conversation with Betty.

"Would you rather I call you Elizabeth now that you've become such a grown up girl?" Mary Anna asked her daughter.

Betty thought for a moment. "Yes, I think so. Elizabeth is a much prettier name. And more grown up."

"When a girl is going on eight years old, she's well on her way to adulthood," Mary Anna smiled. "And you do carry a lot of responsibilities," she added honestly. "Elizabeth it is."

The younger boys began the long journey back to health. Soon they were fussing and crying. "That's the loveliest sound, isn't it?" Mary Anna asked Virginia. There would be no new graves for Daniel to come home to, and Mary Anna gave daily thanks to God for that.

She thought of Daniel all the time, calling him close with her thoughts. She imagined him coming up the road, safe and with the money they needed. His beautiful blue eyes underneath his gray Stetson warmed her. His suntanned face with its hungry mouth moved against her in her thoughts. He would be tall and healthy this time, not sick, like when he had come home from the war. She tingled with the remembrance of him. She ached to hold him and kiss his searching lips.

☙

Daniel estimated they were about four days out of Ellsworth. The men were weary of life on the trail and began talking of being in a real town again; especially when they heard some of the tales Snake and Mac told them about the wide open manner in which cowboys were not only allowed to live, but encouraged.

All Daniel wanted was a bath, a good meal, and a real bed. He made no plans to spend anymore time in Ellsworth than he had to. He and Caleb were planning to turn right around and go home. He suspected Coleman, Mac, and Toad would make the trip with them.

When they could finally see the tiny dots that were the buildings of Ellsworth, Daniel felt as though he were holding the entire herd and all of the men back with his bare hands.

Leaving Coleman in charge, Mac, Caleb, and Daniel left the herd a few miles outside town and went in to strike a bargain with the buyer.

They hadn't ridden far when they were met by a man coming from the direction of Ellsworth.

"Hello, there, and welcome to Ellsworth, center of the cattle industry." He was well dressed and riding a beautiful stallion. "I saw your herd and thought I'd be the first to welcome you."

He rode up even with Daniel. "My name's James P. Quincy. No relation to the president, unfortunately. I'm a cattle buyer." He scanned the distant horizon. "Looks like you have a sizable herd behind you."

When he finally stopped talking, Daniel offered his hand. "I'm Daniel Thornton. This is Caleb West and Mr. MacDonald."

Time must have been money to Mr. Quincy, for he raced on. "I'm here to offer you forty dollars a head." When the men looked at one another, he added, "You won't find a better deal in Ellsworth. I have the cash money in the bank in town. I'll be glad to show it to you."

The price fulfilled Daniel's wildest dreams. He had made a silent agreement with himself that if he could get twenty dollars a head this trip, he'd be overjoyed. Now this man had doubled that! Cattle business was truly a rich man's game. All the long days of danger and boredom had been worth it. He looked over at Caleb, then Mac.

Mac cleared his throat, pointed with his head, and rode off a little way with Daniel following. "He may be all right, but he's the only man we've seen," he whispered. "Cattle could be going for fifty dollars a head. We don't know."

Daniel rode back to the knot of men. "We'll go into town.

I'd like to talk to a few more people."

Mr. Quincy was rubbing his hands together happily. "Let's go. You won't find a better deal. Of that I'm sure." He headed his horse to town. "Supper is on me," he added with a flourish.

They rode in with Mr. Quincy chatting like he was sitting in a front parlor on Sunday. He asked so many questions Daniel was glad when they finally reached the town, for his head hurt from all the talking.

Everything checked out as Mr. Quincy had said it would. The deal was agreed to in principle, leaving only the number of head and the total price to be filled in. Mr. Quincy gave Daniel a large advance, promising to see him after the cattle had been counted and loaded the next day.

"You're a fortunate man, Mr. Thornton. Only a few herds have come in ahead of you. You'll get top dollar. Yes, sir, it truly is the early bird that gets the worm."

That did it for Daniel. He politely thanked Mr. Quincy for the advance, turned down dinner, and headed for the nearest hotel with his two friends, trying to keep his money out of sight as they walked along the muddy boards that served to keep their boots out of the mud.

Suddenly every stranger Daniel saw looked like a robber. They took a room, hurried upstairs, and locked the door. He spread the money out on the bed and the three men stood there staring at it. "I've never seen that much money in my whole life," Daniel breathed.

"Me neither," intoned Caleb.

Mac just shook his head. "And that's only part of it. There's more to come after the cattle are counted and loaded."

"Here, Mac, you take this and go have some fun."

"Yes, sir!" He disappeared like smoke in a high wind.

"You staying in town tonight, Caleb?"

"Virginia'd kill me if I spent more than an hour in this sinful place," he grinned. "I'll go back with you. Maybe tomorrow we can partake of the pleasures of the bathtub and barbers."

"And what a pleasure that'll be," Daniel grinned. "Let's go let the men loose. Those young fellows probably think they're gonna die before they can make it to the city."

Daniel and Caleb stuffed the bills into their saddlebags as covertly as possible.

They were one of the first herds to make it to the rail head. The town had only a few rowdy cowboys making a racket in the saloon near the hotel. Daniel could hear someone beating a tinny piano to death. "Isn't much of a town to brag about, as far as I can see." They mounted up.

"Beats the choices in Stephenville. I count about six saloons. 'Course, they're mostly tents."

"I'd call this town an egg waiting to hatch," Daniel observed. He tipped his hat to an elderly lady walking primly down the planks that served as the sidewalk. Her skirts were dragging in the dust and mud, and she carried a small parasol to guard against the hot evening sun. Her returned smile was slight.

"Don't guess she cottons to cattle barons," Caleb smiled.

"Don't guess we look like cattle barons," argued Daniel.

They eased their mounts down the street. Ellsworth was a roughly built settlement getting ready for prosperity. There was a general store that Daniel marked. He would buy presents for his family there the next day.

He guided his horse around a very young cowboy, staggering down the street glassy-eyed. "I'll bet he doesn't think this was so much fun tomorrow."

Caleb laughed. "The young are so dumb, but I suppose I did the same foolish things."

"Are you confessing?" asked Daniel.

"Nope. Just remembering."

Daniel grinned. "Me, too." He shifted slightly in the saddle. "I'm glad all that nonsense is behind me. I made some bad choices in the past. I don't need the things I thought I did to make me happy. Right at this moment, the only thing that would ake me happier is to be at home with Mary Anna and the kids."

Caleb got a little misty eyed. "Me, too."

Daniel kept a wary eye out as they made their way to the herd and searched in his mind for a place to hide the money.

The men were raring to go. Daniel gave them part of their wages.

Maxwell, Oliver, and Rabbit formed a unit. Two-thirds of the cowboys on the trail were black, freed from the plantations, but they knew there could still be trouble. Even if they stayed at the designated spot for freedmen, there was a high probability of getting into some kind of scrape with some of the white cowboys in town.

Toad and Snake rode up and joined them. One by one the other men did, too. They were going in together, and they would take care of each other like family on this night of celebration. They had been forged into a family by the drive, and they rode out as one.

Coleman hung back. "I don't have a hankering to go spend my wages on foolishness. Reckon you could use some help holding the herd."

"Be back by sunup," Daniel shouted to the men as they rode off. "We've got a herd to move into town tomorrow." He hoped at least one of the men had heard him.

It was right at sunup when the party goers dragged up. Oliver and Mac were the only ones smiling. Mac was riding beside Toad, holding him onto his horse. Toad's face was the color of the amphibian for which he was named. Snake's eyes held a glazed look, but he was sitting straight in the saddle.

"I had a grand time," bubbled Maxwell. "We found this man that played the piano in this place. Stayed there all night long, singin' and laughin'. I never had so much fun!" He laughed. "You should have seen old Toad doing that Irish jig."

"Course, he ain't dancing much right now," commented Snake.

"You look like you could use some of the hair of the snake that bit you," Toad said in a slurred voice.

The chuck wagon was already packed and the men had to do without coffee or restorative food. "It's a good thing we're only a mile or so out of town," Daniel told Coleman as he watched the men cling to their saddles. He strongly disapproved of their behavior, but he knew only time and experience would cure intemperance. He was mad at them for not being in top shape for the last of the drive but grinned at the knowledge that their bodies would punish them far more severely than he ever could.

There was some evidence to support the claim that they had all had a bath, and they were freshly shorn, but they were a motley-looking bunch right now.

Daniel rode to the point to talk with Mac. "Drive 'em up to the pens by the rail head. When it comes time to counting the herd, I want you right there for our tally. You'd better have Maxwell do the white marking. We're definitely short-handed this morning. Toad or Snake would probably fall off the fence." Daniel was to find that tallying the cattle was considered one step below riding drag. Two men sat at the mouth of the cattle car. One counted and one marked the cattle on the rump with white. It would be a hot day, and the cattle were packed tightly on top of one another, their nervous droppings stamped by their hooves to release the pungent smell. The dust was almost unbearable. It would take many hours to send the herd through the chute one at a time. But it was too important a job to leave to a careless hand. Every cow counted was money in their pockets.

Daniel stood on the side of the pens and looked with pride at the herd they had brought in all the way from Erath County, Kansas. It had been an enormous risk, but they had made it. The full extent of the new wealth he had just earned had not yet penetrated, but he was excited by the entire venture.

By noon the heat at the pens had become so oppressive that Daniel sent for Coleman to spell Mac and had Oliver come to do the marking. When Mac climbed down from the top rail, he strolled over to Daniel.

"You did a good job, Mac," Daniel noted. Now that he understood how dirty a job counting was, he added, "There's a big bonus in it for you."

Mac smiled. He took off his bandana and leaned on the rail with Daniel. "Gives a man a good feeling to see all these cows, don't it? Sort of righteous or something." He fumbled with his feelings, but Daniel knew what he meant.

"Yeah." They exchanged broad smiles.

Caleb, who had been on the other side of the huge pens, came up to join them. "Don't seem real," he said as he shook his head in disbelief. Then he slapped Daniel on the back. "We made it, Dan, we made it!"

And then they were standing in the bank once more with

the tally from both sides, splitting the difference in the number counted. Daniel finished the paperwork. Mr. Quincy withdrew the rest of the money and handed the large stack to Daniel. Shaking Daniel's hand, he repeated his desire to work with them next year and left with all parties satisfied.

Daniel divided the money roughly in half and stuck it in Caleb's hands. "Here we go again." He eyed the other people in the bank and didn't see anyone paying attention to them.

"I hadn't thought about this part of it. Protecting the cash, I mean," said Caleb.

"We'll think of something, Caleb."

"Onliest place I know that's big enough to take care of this bundle is in here," he said as he removed his hat and stuffed the money into the crown. He settled the hat back on his head firmly and looked at Daniel. "Okay?"

"Okay. Until you meet a lady," he laughed.

"Don't think there's much danger of that in this town." He offered his arm to Daniel. "Shall we repair to the baths, Sir Daniel?"

Daniel struck his arm through Caleb's. "Let's, Sir Caleb. I told the butler of the baths to have them ready for us."

But no matter how relaxed Daniel became, he never took his eyes off the two hats sitting carelessly on the wooden crates beside the tubs.

"Caleb, I'm going to buy my land up on the North Bosque and build that mansion for Mary Anna."

Caleb considered this. "Okay. I'll buy the land next to it. Guess I should build a mansion, too, for Virginia." He sighed deeply, inhaling the warm smell of fresh soap. "We've come a long way, Dan. A long way since the war."

Daniel rose and stood on the wooden slats. He poured fresh hot water over himself to rinse off and began toweling off his slender frame.

Caleb noted the stark contrast between Daniel's sun-browned hands and face and his white body. He laughed. "You look like a lily with brown leaves."

"Look who's talking. Come on, you lazy hound dog, let's go get us the best food this town has to offer."

It wasn't hard to find that. There was only one café in Ellsworth, and the food gave both men indigestion. It was heavy and greasy and sat like a stone in Daniel's stomach. "I'll die soon if I don't get some of Mary Anna's cooking," he moaned.

They left the café, noted Rabbit was getting the supply wagon reloaded, and entered the store to buy gifts for their loved ones. Daniel got a pretty gold necklace with a small ruby in it for Mary Anna, a finely worked gold ring for Betty, and pocketknives for the boys. "One last thing," he said to the storekeeper. "Do you have any peppermint?" He felt a little dizzy at spending so much money so quickly, but he reminded himself there was plenty left.

Caleb and Daniel went back to the hotel and got another room. Daniel sat down with contentment on the lumpy bed. "This will sure feel good tonight."

Caleb had a frown on his forehead. "The money. Where will we hide it?"

"We'll put it all over everywhere, so if they find one stash they may think that's all there is," said Daniel.

When they dressed the next day, they stuffed cash in their pockets, the tops of their socks, inside their hats, and in the supply wagon for the long trip home.

It was getting colder by the day, and Daniel wanted nothing to stop his trip home. He was taking a huge present to the woman he loved.

five

Mary Anna looked off in the distance. Riders were approaching. Squinting her eyes for a clearer view, she identified a chuck wagon and two riders. Daniel! Minutes later, the small party rode up, and Daniel sprang from his horse to fold Mary Anna in his arms. Her heart sang with joy that Daniel was safe at home in her arms, hugging her tightly. Tears of happiness slid down her face, but she made no attempt to wipe them away.

Daniel tipped her head back to look at the face he had conjured up in his dreams so many times on the drive and kissed the mouth for which he had hungered. "You're even more beautiful than I remembered," he whispered. Then someone kicked him in the stomach. He grinned at Mary Anna. "Guess that baby doesn't want to share you with me."

"She's just letting you know she's glad you're home," smiled Mary Anna.

The warmth of the cabin and the greeting Daniel received made his face shine. He gave out the presents, saving Mary Anna's for last.

"Oh, it's lovely," she breathed. "I'll wear it always as a reminder of this day."

"They didn't have any diamonds up there," he apologized, "but I am going to give you the other present. I'm buying the land, and we'll build a mansion on it." He stood prouder than any peacock that ever spread its massive fan of fancy feathers.

"You're a cattleman," she grinned. "Land owner and all."

"The Lord has delivered us to the Land of Milk and Honey at last."

Mary Anna's face was still glowing. "Oh, Daniel, the Lord has been so good to us. I know all of it could be gone in a minute, but I'm just beside myself with happiness. I never thought it would be this easy!"

"Easy!" exclaimed Daniel, "You should have been there." He thought of the cyclone. "You're right about how fast it could all be gone. But I want to bask in the glory of the blessings He's given us." His eyes were full of love for her and his voice begged her to rejoice with him.

"How can I say no to you when you look at me like that?" she said. "Tonight will be unbridled joy, and tomorrow we'll be sober about all our new responsibilities."

The next day Daniel groomed himself carefully and went to buy the land. He returned that evening with the deed for 1,250 acres of prime land, and Mary Anna thought she would have to buy him a new hat to fit his head, now swollen with pride.

"We have the dream in our hands," she said softly as he handed her the deed.

She rose from her chair, holding the paper. "Yes. But now what will we do with it?"

"Use it for us and our children, and anyone else we choose." He came to her and put his arms around her while she rested her head on his chest.

"Are we different now?" she asked.

Daniel was quiet for a long while. "Yes and no. I don't want the love between us to change or anything bad to happen to our children. I want us all to stay as happy as we are now. And yet, it feels wonderful not to have to worry if I'll be able to take care of you all. I know I could lose all this wealth today. I don't want it to control our lives. But I want to use it. I believe the Lord has blessed us so we can be a blessing to others. I want to use it to build a place where all our children can grow up and marry and bring their children back to visit. A center for our world. We have the money to let our children be anything they want to be. We're free to choose."

He held her closer. "But if I have to choose between our love and the money, I'd give the money away in a second." He held her away from him slightly. "Never doubt that," he said. And gently he took her face in his hands and kissed her mouth as he had when they were first married.

"I never dreamed my life could be so happy," Mary Anna sighed. "I didn't think a love like this could exist. I never saw it before. And sometimes I'm so happy, it frightens me. Like now. Hold me a little tighter so I won't be scared."

"I believe everything you said, right up to the 'hold me a little tighter so I won't be scared.' I don't think you're afraid of anything," laughed Daniel.

She gazed unseeingly off into the distance. "Yes, I am. But tonight is not the time to speak of them."

Mary Anna knew there would be pain and heartache in their lives. There had to be, for that was life. She only hoped she would be strong enough to meet the tests she felt sure were to come with living out the dream. When she went to bed that night, she spent extra time in prayer. And Annah kicked within her, full of life and mischief.

❧

Annah chose to arrive on January 7, a cold and snowy day.

From the moment the baby was laid in her arms, Mary Anna was enchanted. Annah was somehow the embodiment of her parents' dream, a promise for the future of which they had spoken. While Mary Anna loved all her children, somehow Annah seemed to be the child of her heart. In those secret moments when no one was around, she let the full measure of her love fall on Annah without reservation.

Elizabeth was delighted with her sister. "She finally got here. When will she be able to play dolls with me?"

"Not for a while," her mother answered with a kiss to Elizabeth's forehead.

Elizabeth solved the problem herself. She made Annah the doll, dressing her, playing with her, and taking care of her endlessly. "She's a real doll, isn't she, Mama?" And Mary Anna laughed.

During the winter the men rounded up more cattle and mustangs as they ran across them on the winter pastures. The herd was beginning to grow again.

One morning the day dawned brightly making the sky a cerulean bowl.

It was so clear that they could see the Palo Pinto Mountains dotting the western horizon. Even the air seemed warmer as Daniel brought up water for the cabin from the stream. It was a perfect day. But toward noon the wind picked up from the north and developed a decided bite.

The men complained of the dropping temperature when they came in for lunch. When Thaddeus came thumping in he said, "My bad leg tells me we're in for one big blow." By one o'clock, the north sky was deep blue.

"We're in for it now," Daniel said, casting a look over his shoulders. "Better get the horses up toward the barn," he instructed the men, "there's a Blue Northern blowing in. We're likely to have snow by supper time."

Everything was battened down and extra firewood added to the pile by the door. By four o'clock, the temperature had fallen drastically.

Mary Anna prepared supper for the men, and they came in out of the weather gratefully.

"Can we do sledding?" asked Peter with shining eyes.

"Me, too," chimed in Elizabeth.

The boys ignored her. "Can we, Mama?" they asked again.

"Let's wait and see if it comes before I make any promises," she hedged.

"Snow may be good for the kids, but it's murder on the stock," grumbled Toad.

When Coleman and Toad left for their bunkhouse, huge, fluffy flakes had already begun drifting down. The children were dancing in their excitement. They put on their coats and ran outside, lifting their arms trying to catch the flakes.

By the next morning, the snow was over Daniel's boots that he wore when he went out to check the barn. Coleman, Toad, and Thaddeus were throwing hay out into the snow for the other animals.

The children were content to run out and play for a few minutes and then come in to the warmth of the fire. To keep them occupied, Mary Anna read to them. Daniel enjoyed listening to Mary Anna read in the long evenings. He was a pretty good reader himself, but Mary Anna had never given up her love of reading, no matter how busy she was. Under her tutelage, the children were doing well with their own reading skills.

"I don't want them to grow up ignorant." It was a point of pride for her that everyone in their family could read. Even the little boys were getting their first lessons. Thaddeus was good about helping them.

"Someday we'll have a proper school again," Mary Anna dreamed.

The wind grew more fierce during the night, and the storm continued without letup for days. When the storm finally blew itself out, several feet of snow covered the ground. No one went outside except to feed the animals.

When the temperature finally allowed some of the snow to begin melting, Daniel took the two older boys hunting. They felled a deer.

"Good shot, Tump. That's a nice fat buck." They were just inside the first good stand of trees beyond the river.

"Papa," Peter said in a frightened voice.

Daniel looked up just as low growls began in the throat of the leader of a pack of timber wolves.

"They must be starved," Daniel said quietly. "Tump, get ready. If they charge us, I'll shoot the leader. You get the one right behind him and don't stop firing." He could see the boys were terrified. "They'll turn tail and run if we kill the leader," he assured them.

The wolves were still growling, poised in attack posture. Daniel waited, sighting the leader's head carefully. The wolf was large and heavily muscled. Long fangs showed through his open mouth. Daniel hoped the pack could be bluffed into leaving, but he saw the muscles of the lead animal tensing. The leader's eyes glinted yellow and cold. Daniel waited only a fraction of a second before he squeezed the trigger. The wolf sprung just as he fired, and it fell instantly dead into the snow, its blood staining the white blanket. Tump fired before the report of Daniel's rifle had stopped. He wounded the second animal and Peter finished him off with his shot. Daniel dropped the third one, and as Peter shot at the fourth animal, the rest of the pack made a quick retreat.

"Let's get this buck out of here," Daniel instructed. "They'll be back. They're too hungry not to give it another try." They draped the buck over Peter's horse, and he rode double with his brother.

"Will they follow us?" Peter shouted.

"Maybe." That thought hurried everyone along.

That night as the Thorntons ate roasted venison, they could hear mournful cries echoing across the moonlit land.

Peter shivered. "I'm glad we live in a strong house."

"Me, too, son," his father said. But until the deep winter eased, hunting would be an even more dangerous venture.

Slowly the winter loosened its unkind grip and the spring activities began again.

Daniel was especially pleased with Tump's uncanny ability with horses. He was good at making friends with them and coaxing them to let him on their backs.

One day Tump was trying to work with a horse the men had brought in. The horse had a glazed look in his eyes and his ears were always pointed. This was not a good sign. Tump managed to get the bit in the horse's mouth, but when the time came for the saddle, it was a different thing all together.

As soon as Tump put the saddle on the horse's back, the horse fell over onto his back and lay there.

"What in the world!" said Tump. By now Toad had come in to witness this strange spectacle. Tump took off the saddle and the horse stood up.

"Never saw a horse do that before," puzzled Toad.

"Whoa, boy," said Tump silkily. He stroked the horse's head. "It's only a saddle. It won't hurt you." He eased the saddle back onto the horse, and the animal promptly threw himself on his back again, lying there calmly.

He called his father to the barn to witness this new horse's antics.

Once again when the saddle was placed on his back, the

horse fell down and lay on his back.

Daniel burst out laughing. "A falling-down horse?" he said. "Never have I ever seen that."

Coleman and Mac were consulted.

"That creature is purely stupid," was Mac's assessment.

"Or purely smart," quipped Tump.

"Better let that one alone. We've got too many good animals for you to waste time with that one," Daniel told Tump.

Reluctantly Tump turned the horse back into the pasture and began working with another one. But the odd behavior of the first horse poked at him. He'd never had a horse he couldn't do something with, and this was a real challenge.

At different times he'd try unsuccessfully to get the horse to accept the saddle.

"Looks like you're going to have a long day," Toad laughed from the top rail of the corral.

"Don't you have anything to do but sit there and watch me?" complained Tump irritably.

"I'm giving you moral support," replied Toad. "Some advice, too. I talked to some of the other men, and they gave me some ideas. I'm here to give you some of their horse wisdom."

They hobbled the horse so he couldn't buck without falling down, and snubbed his head to a post, so he endured the blanket Tump put on him. But when Tump untied his head, he could swear he saw a gleam in the animal's eyes as he threw his head around and pulled the blanket off with his teeth.

"Hey, Tump, I think you've finally got a horse that's smarter than you." Toad was having a fine time watching the boy struggle with the stubborn animal.

Doggedly Tump snubbed the horse's head close to the post

again, but not before the animal managed to nip the back of his pants. The trick caused Toad to fall off the rail with laughter.

Tump rubbed the painful nip and looked into the horse's big brown eyes. "You've had the last laugh this time, but I will get a blanket on you yet."

Mary Anna put ointment on the painful bite and Tump sat crooked in his chair at supper that night.

The next day Daniel told him, "I'm sure that with enough time you'll be able to break the falling-down horse. But your time is better spent working with the other horses. I'm afraid by the time you do break him, you'll find out he's too dumb to do anything. Just let the horse be. One of the sad facts of life is that a man can't always be successful, even at what he's good at. Just let him be. It'll make a good story to tell your grandchildren," he grinned.

At the end of April, Mary Anna was greatly embarrassed to find herself pregnant again. "I can't be again so soon," she wailed to Daniel. "I'm not ready for another baby."

Daniel was completely confused by Mary Anna's lack of joy.

Virginia comforted her. But by May, Mary Anna was huge.

"Virginia," she said as they spun the cotton into thread and wrapped it in big balls, "I shouldn't be this large so soon. Do you think it's because I'm not recovered from Anna's birth?"

Virginia wrinkled her eyebrows and measured Mary Anna with her eyes. "Hmm. You are big," she agreed. "There's only one thing that could cause that, Mary Anna, and you know it." She grinned widely.

"Don't even think it!" groaned Mary Anna. "You were supposed to say what I wanted you to." She put her face over her hands and moaned. "Not twins! I couldn't survive carrying them, much less taking care of them!"

Virginia knelt down beside Mary Anna. "My dear, twins are special. I know that it's not often they both survive, but you're strong and healthy, and you have a lot of people to help you. Let's rejoice that the Lord has chosen you to be these babies' mother. And let's pray that they both live to celebrate your one hundredth birthday."

Quietly Mary Anna said, "You're a good friend, Virginia. If I have a girl, I'll name her for you."

News of the coming twins spread rapidly among the cowboys and then to Stephenville. Mary Anna had never received so much pampering. She knew that the longer she carried the babies, the better chance they had to live, so she took all the advice and all the pampering given her.

Daniel wanted to begin building the new house right away. He was full of plans and excitement. Mary Anna refused to talk about it.

"But you said as soon as Annah was here, we'd get started," he protested.

"And now I'm carrying two babies, and I really don't want to discuss it. I don't have the energy for it." She tried to rearrange her body in the rocking chair to a more comfortable position.

"But you don't have to do the building!" Daniel insisted.

"If you're going to build me a grand house, I want to supervise every nail that's put in it. Men know nothing about kitchens and the little things that make a house so convenient. We're fine here. And safe." Her voice left no room for argument.

"Daniel," she added softly, "while I was sitting by the window looking at the woods two days ago, I saw the silhouette of a man. I'm sure I did. It was an Indian. I could tell because of the shadow of his hair. He was watching us. Before I could call for anyone he disappeared."

Daniel tried to calm her fears. "He was probably looking for game."

"No, you know he wasn't. He was watching us." She shivered. "And even from that long way away, I could feel death radiating from him. Anger and death. I don't want to leave this safe little fort we have here with the Wests until Santana, Tall Tree, and Ten Bears are no longer a threat to us. If we build the house now, they'll burn us out more easily. Kill us, if they can. They're desperate, cornered people, and they are fighting to survive just as we are."

Daniel looked at her earnest face and heard the wisdom in her words. "I wish you had told me earlier about the man in the woods. I would have posted a guard." His words were gentle. "It's a test of having the dream, isn't it, to have the money to do it, and yet have to wait?"

"I think maybe it is."

"Well, the money isn't going anywhere unless there's a bank robbery." He thought of the big bank in Fort Worth where he had deposited his money. "It's in as safe a place as it can be." He sighed deeply. "All right. We'll wait. I hope I don't have to get a badge and go out and catch those renegades myself."

"I doubt you will, my love. You'll be too busy building up some other part of your kingdom."

Daniel took to heart what she said and began planting orchards of peach trees and larger fields of wheat and cotton. Then he hired more men to help him with those crops.

In spite of all their night guards, horses and a few cattle continued to disappear in lieu of all out raids.

Coleman came in one morning with a large, silly grin on

his face.

Daniel raised his eyebrows quizzically. "Yes?"

"Remember the falling-down horse? One of the braves tried to steal him last night. I heard the dogs and went out to check, and I saw him slide on the horse's back. That stupid horse rolled over just like a dog wanting his stomach scratched. Near smashed that Indian. I was laughing so hard I couldn't hardly get a bead on him. Guess it was just one man, and he didn't get anything but embarrassment. Bet he's a mite more careful about which horse he tries to take out of here next time."

Daniel laughed heartily as he imagined the sight, but the incident reminded him again that they were still in danger. Mary Anna's advice sounded wiser every day.

He did pick up two hopeful pieces of information when he went into Stephenville. In March, Texas had been re-admitted to the Union by President Grant and twenty companies of Rangers were to be sent to protect the frontier.

Daniel's hope rose for building the house soon. "With all those men, we'll be rid of the Indian problem in no time," he told Charlie.

He told Mary Anna the good news as soon as he got home, expecting her to relent about building the house.

"No. Let's see the Indians gone first." She was steadfast in her feelings.

Caleb and Virginia came over after supper, and the men sat outside in the lovely spring night, talking about Daniel's news.

"It's all paid off, hasn't it, Dan?" Caleb gloated. Then he turned sober. "When you and Mary Anna do decide to build the new house, I am thinking seriously about moving Virginia and me into town. I don't think I want to be a cattle baron now. I want to be a town baron and maybe build a house bigger than anyone else's."

"And not have to fight the Indians," Daniel added.

"And not have to fight the Indians," Caleb agreed. "I'm getting too old for all of that. Time for me to sit back and watch my kids grow." He took a deep breath. "Just smell that air." He smiled broadly. "It belongs to you while it's blowing over this land."

"I doubt that," Daniel laughed. "But I sure do enjoy it all the same." He turned serious. "You've heard about the political stuff that's going on?"

"Only about Texas being readmitted and the Rangers coming," Caleb said.

"The radical Republicans have won, and the new constitution has been ratified. But they filled all the offices with extremists." Daniel shook his head. "Texas is wide open for everything. Even Governor Davis has been accused of fraud, and the state police are making a mess of their job. Charlie had a copy of the *Tri Weekly Gazette* from Waco. Headlines said there was a riot and the sheriff called in the U.S. troops to put it down. I don't know if living in town is going to be so peaceful."

"It will be in Stephenville," Caleb said confidently.

Inside Virginia and Mary Anna were discussing things from the feminine point of view.

"You'll be happy in town, Virginia." Mary Anna was lying in bed, sewing tiny stitches in baby clothes, while Virginia readied the smaller children for bed and shooed the older ones up into the sleeping loft.

"Yes. I'm looking forward to it." She finally came over and sat in the chair beside Mary Anna's bed. "You feeling all right?"

Mary Anna sighed happily. "I have never enjoyed a pregnancy so much. All I do all day long is take care of Annah and then give her to Elizabeth to play with. I've made so many baby clothes. The way everyone treats me, you'd think I'd never had a child before."

"Well, not twins," Virginia added. "What do you think they'll be?"

"One of each would be nice."

"Take off your wedding ring," Virginia commanded. She got a sewing thread, put it through the gold circle, and hung it over Mary Anna's ample middle. "If it swings to and fro it will be boys. If it goes in a circle, it will be girls."

Breathlessly they wait for the ring to move. Subtly it began making the motion of a pendulum.

"Boys!" they said together.

"Do you really think that works?" Mary Anna asked.

"It works half the time," Virginia grinned. "Time will tell."

"Well, I certainly have a lot of that," Mary Anna said in a half cheerful voice.

And they were long days. Soon even sitting in her rocker brought on contractions, and she was confined to bed. This only gave her more time to think about the absence of Indian attacks and fret about when the next one might come.

When she mentioned her fears to Daniel, he said, "They've been very busy in other parts of the county. Santana, Lone Wolf, and Kicking Bird haven't given up, they've just relocated."

"Kicking Bird? Who in the world is that?"

"Kiowa. He and Lone Wolf have joined forces now." He smoothed her hair against her damp forehead. "Don't worry about them. Just be glad they are causing their trouble in other places. Why, they probably took one look at our fortress and decided to try for easier game."

She thought he was probably right.

By late September, the men were through with the roundup and branding. They were running late this year, and that worried Daniel. Being first was important.

Mac would head up the drive. The men were constantly on guard, even though they suspected that trouble had moved out of the area for a while.

There was no thought of Caleb going on this cattle drive; he had made that clear. But Daniel was like an old hunting dog that saw his master take out the gun and then told the old dog to stay home. There was so much to hate about the drive, and so much to love. Daniel had two babies that would come when Mary Anna could carry them no longer. That could be any day. He knew where he belonged, but he couldn't quell his desires to be out on the trail.

Tump approached him. "I want to go with the men. Before you say no, remember that some day I'll be a cattleman just like you, and I'll need to know all the things you know. I'll be careful, and I'll be with men you trust." He left nothing for Daniel to say, so Daniel just nodded his head.

The day finally arrived. Daniel hugged his son good-bye and then spoke to Coleman and Mac.

"The Lord be with you, men," Daniel said as he shook their hands.

"He will be," said Coleman. "Tump will be fine, Captain."

"Take care of Miss Mary Anna," said Mac. "And tell her we're real proud of her." They tipped their hats to Caleb as he rode by them to Daniel.

With a huge mixture of feelings careening through his chest, Daniel watched the herd move out.

Caleb spoke the words for him. "I feel like the girl that got left home from the party." He frowned. "I didn't want to feel that way."

"I know. Come on, Caleb. I'll buy you a cup of coffee." They headed for the cabin, and as they walked into the kitchen area, Virginia yelled at them, "It's time! The babies are on the way! Put the water on to boil! And stay out of my way!"

It was the end of September, and Mary Anna had successfully carried the babies eight months. When Virginia finally stuck her head out of the cabin, her smile told the whole story. "Two fine, boys, Daniel. Good and healthy boys." She stepped back to let Daniel to the bedside.

"I want to call them Arthur and Oscar," said Mary Anna. "The one with the red thread is Arthur. He was born first." She smiled tiredly at Daniel. "I just couldn't name them Jacob and Esau."

"Arthur and Oscar are good strong names, family names." Gently he kissed her on the forehead and then touched the hand of each little boy. "Thank You, Lord, that You've given us two more fine sons. And that my Mary Anna is safe." He didn't try to hide the tears in his eyes.

He heard Virginia say to Caleb, "I'd better get my sewing thread ready. He's likely not to have a button left on that coat by the time he tells everyone about his little boys." There was no mistaking the joy behind Virginia's gruff voice.

All the next day the family took turns peeking at the tiny bundles sleeping in their mother's bed. Their cradles were ready, and they would go in them, but not yet.

Every time she looked at the scrunched up faces, Mary Anna thanked God. And she learned to tell their personalities almost at once. She didn't need the colored thread after a few days. But everyone else did.

six

Daniel, Caleb, and Thaddeus worked the crops while the men were on the trail drive. It was a fairly successful crop. Daniel was feeling good about all the money that would be coming in this year. He would be set solid for a long time. His lips parted in a grimy smile as the last of the hay was stored in the barn.

Lieutenant Mooreland came by to pick up a few more horses. "You do have the best horses in the county," he complimented Daniel.

"Careful breeding and tending," Daniel answered with a smile. He had come to like this brusk young man trying to do an impossible job with too few men and too much territory.

Lieutenant Mooreland and his men stayed for dinner. After the good meal, he said, "I dislike telling you this more than I can say, but you need to know so you'll be prepared. Santana, Big Tree, Satank, and 150 of their men raided a ten-wagon train. I can't tell you how bad it was. They just missed ambushing General Sheridan. Also the Lee family of six was wiped out, and Mr. Dobs, the Justice of the Peace of Palo Pinto County was murdered. Scalped and his ears and nose cut off."

Mary Anna felt faint.

"We've reached the point where everyone has agreed the peace treaties are not working. We're actively looking for the men to arrest them."

"I didn't think you could arrest reservation Indians," Daniel said.

"Normally we can't. But this is too big to be ignored. The men will be arrested and stand trial. If we can find them," he added. "So be on your guard. The wagon trail was between Fort Richardson and Fort Belnap."

Daniel and Mary Anna exchanged looks of fear. Fort Belnap was about fifteen miles north.

Lieutenant Mooreland was back a few days later with more news. This time there was a big grin on his face. "They got 'em. The trial will be at Jacksboro. It'll be the first time a reservation Indian has ever been tried." Something akin to hope glimmered from his eyes. "The public outrage has demanded the government do something about the depredations of the Indians." He saluted smartly and wheeled his horse, off on more patrols.

Mary Anna sat down at the table and smoothed the calico tablecloth. "I thought I had come to terms with the Indians and the whites. I've always felt sorry for them, that we pushed them off their land. They're a noble people, and yet I simply can't understand the way they wantonly kill."

Daniel sat down with her. In his blue eyes smoldered anger. "I'm the one who thought the only good Indian was a dead Indian. Then I saw them as a people, living pretty much the same way we do. I fight for my land, and I can understand their fight for their land. But why do they kill everything that gets in their way? Even in the war we didn't kill anybody but the men in uniform. At least we didn't try to." He shook his head. "I want to hate them again. It was easier that way. But now I can't." He looked sad. "I'm angry with them, hate what they do, but I can't know how they must feel inside to make them do these things."

When he knew the trial should be over, Daniel was so anxious to know the outcome that he went in to Stephenville to the general store.

"You ain't gonna like what I have to say," Charlie warned him.

"They're going to hang them, aren't they?"

"Nope. Thomas Ball and J. A. Woolfork of Weatherford did their best to get them off, but the court gave 'em the death sentence anyway.

"But that's what we wanted," said a confused Daniel.

"Yeah, but Santana and Big Tree's sentence was commuted to life imprisonment. Court said as long as the Kiowas behaved and stayed on the reservations, they would just keep them in jail."

"That makes no sense at all!" exploded Daniel. "That's not going to slow down those Indians!"

Charlie nodded in agreement. "Onliest thing I can figure out is that they're trying to avoid an all-out war. Maybe they think if they kill the chiefs, their braves would just rally and raid worse."

"Cutting off the head of a rattler is usually a good way to slow down his tail," Daniel commented bitterly.

"Guess they're afraid this snake has more than one head."

"Quannah Parker?"

Charlie nodded again. "Could be since he's half-breed, he has more to prove?"

"No, it's because his father was Nocona." Anger glinted in Daniel's eyes. "This is one big mistake, and we're going to pay the consequences for it."

"You too mad to buy anything?" Charlie asked pragmatically.

"Don't think my mad spell would be a good enough

excuse to Mary Anna for not buying what she needs." Daniel took out the list he was carrying in his vest and handed it to Charlie. He stewed the entire time it was being filled and went home angry.

Back at the ranch there was agreement that the trial had turned out all wrong. And they were frightened by feared retaliations.

"In a way, it's the worst thing they could have done to those chiefs." Mary Anna thought of the vast stretches of prairie they had roamed. "Being cooped up in a jail, like that. I don't think they're afraid of death. They'd be heroes then, but it's a disgrace for them to be kept in a cage."

"I think you're right," Caleb said, "but the bottom line is that we ain't ever gonna be safe until them Indians are put somewhere else."

Daniel's anger grew in proportion to the support he found for his views. All he had ever wanted was to make a living. The Indians' sole purpose in life was to make this impossible for him. Now the government had betrayed him. A government he didn't want, one which he had fought against. And now his own wife was taking up for their enemy.

He jerked his hat off the peg by the door and stomped out. The embarrassed silence that he left behind was not broken. People slid out of sight. The discussion of the trial and its outcome was over.

ta

Word about Mary Anna's skills as a midwife began to spread around. More settlers were moving in, and when a frantic husband showed up at her door, she gladly went with him. Daniel always made one of the men accompany her if he couldn't go.

It also became commonplace for the men to come to Mary

Anna for stitching up a bad cut or for her to prescribe something from her medicine cabinet for their various ailments. She had a natural instinct for diagnosing and even helped with the stock once in a while.

She was also looking for her son to come home from the drive any day now. When the cloud of dust surrounding a group of riders finally was sighted, she waited anxiously until she could make out Tump's figure on Thunder.

Daniel pounded him on the back, but Tump had to tell him, "We didn't get there first. We didn't do as good as you and Mr. West did." There was sorrow in his face.

"Whatever it is, it was worth the drive, and I'm proud of you, son." He pounded Tump on the back and then gave him a big bear hug. "I'm so proud of you," he echoed.

Peter was glad to see his brother again, but tried hard not to be jealous of all the attention Tump was getting from their father. He had worked hard this summer, and he knew his father appreciated that, but he had never pounded him on the back or given him a bear hug. He made up his mind right then and there that he would be on the next drive, even if he had to sneak off to go.

Daniel further honored his son by asking him to go to Ft. Worth to deposit the money. Then he asked Peter to accompany him. "You boys will be running this ranch some day. I'll be sitting on the porch swing, and I don't want you asking me what to do with the million dollars you made on the drive," he grinned.

Peter was mollified, and Tump regaled him with stories of the drive all the way to the bank and back. "You'll be on the next one, Peter. I'll need you." And he gave his brother his best brotherly smile.

Seven-year-old Henry looked up to his big brothers. He

copied everything they did. He wanted to be a cowboy and go on the drive with them. He knew they wouldn't let him go for a long time, so he played cowboy every day, practicing for the time when he could go.

He watched the men, too, and the one that caught his eye was Snake. Snake had come back from this drive with a new collection of snakeskins. He wore a hat with a rattlesnake skin wrapped around the crown, the rattles hanging down along the brim. His belt was of rattlesnake skin, and even the sheath in which he carried his skinning knife was made of snakeskin.

The women wouldn't go near Snake, but Henry admired his bravery, which he attributed to killing all those snakes.

A few days later Mary Anna was feeding the family when she noticed a very unpleasant smell. She was relatively sure something had crawled up under the cabin again and died. She reminded herself to say something to Daniel about it. Each day she would smell the offensive odor, but Daniel couldn't find a cause for it. It seemed to come and go. But when it was around, it was awful.

On Saturday it was terrible, and it got noticeably stronger when Willie and Henry came in for their scrubbing.

"Can't we go down to the river and scrub, Mama?" complained Henry.

"Absolutely not. I want you clean enough for church. Here, let me help you with your shirt, Henry." As she leaned close to him, the smell almost knocked her over. "What in the world!" she said as she lifted his long-tailed shirt.

"Isn't it beautiful?" bragged Henry of his belt. "I caught a snake and killed him and skinned him just like Mr. Snake did."

"Henry!"

"It wasn't poisonous, Mama," he protested as she took the belt from him with two fingers.

"Neither has the skin been cured and tanned properly. It's absolutely rotten!" She opened the door and threw the belt as far away as she could, almost vomiting at the smell. "Next time you want a snakeskin belt, young man," she ordered as she scrubbed him bright red, "you ask your father the right way to do it!"

Daniel roared with laughter when she told him the tale.

"You wouldn't have thought it so funny if you'd been the one to dispose of that rotten mess," she complained. "Those boys will be the death of me yet," she sighed. But privately she smiled at Henry's ingenuity at acquiring something he really wanted.

Daniel wanted something, too. Since he wasn't actively going on the drives, he thought seriously about running for county commissioner. His lodge brothers were encouraging. Stephenville was becoming quite a little town, though it would never fit the description of a boom town.

A clapboard church had been built, and more stores were going into business. More houses appeared around the square of the courthouse.

When Daniel rode into town, he was greeted by many friends. He made a point of meeting the new people in town, too. In spite of that, he came back to the ranch on election day with a long face.

"Oh, darling, I'm so sorry. You'll get it next time," Mary Anna said confidently.

"I'm not so sure there will be a next time," Daniel said in a gruff voice.

"Of course there will be."

Daniel had a hard time settling down to ranch work for a while, then soothed his dented pride with the purchase of land that brought his holdings up to 3,300 acres. He mentioned the house again to Mary Anna.

"Not until the Indians are gone," she said firmly. She looked into his eyes. "You heard the same rumor I did. The Indians are massing for an all-out attack. We're in more danger than ever."

"If the meeting President Grant called with all the chiefs in St. Louis doesn't work, I don't know what will happen." He sighed. "I'm not getting my hopes up, but maybe it's a start." For their protection, he hired on more men. He would be ready when the time came.

As though to prove her point, a few nights later they were raided. The children's favorite pet colt refused to leave, and the Indians shot it through the heart with an arrow.

Amid the sobbing children, Mary Anna took one look at the dead colt and knew the story of Thunder's recovery was not to be repeated.

Rarely did a week pass without some losses to the Indians by someone in the area. Daniel wrestled with the question of whether or not he should make a drive that fall.

He and Caleb discussed it over apple pie and hot coffee.

"I'm agin it, Dan. Competition is getting rougher."

"I thought of driving them up there and wintering them, but that blizzard last year wiped out a lot of men. On the other hand, that should pump up the market price."

"We can still run our cattle together up there. 'Course we'll need a traveling brand now. Rustling is getting to be as big a problem as the Indians."

"Comanches and Kiowas are still raiding off the Ft. Sill Reservation." Daniel punched his fork hard into the piece of pie. "Isn't it ever going to end?"

"Eventually. We're crowding them out with more settlers every day. We can't kill them all, so we'll muscle them off the land, I reckon."

Daniel still had men out on night guard for the cattle and horses. Sometimes they lost a few head in the night, but they never knew for sure when there would be an all out attack.

Toad was out with the men one night. The cattle were acting nervous, and Toad pulled out a harmonica and played "Aura Lee" for them. It made him edgy for the cattle to be spooky. His horse shied at the slightest thing, and Toad felt himself straining to hear and identify each sound.

He put his hand on his revolver, reassuring himself it was there and fully loaded. Then he checked to see if his rifle was in its leather holster, hanging down beside the pommel of the saddle. He kept constant check on where the other men were.

It was a clear night, the stars blazing down in all their glory, and the wind barely stirring the rich blades of grass, but it was not peaceful.

Toad was ready. He had felt this all before. He knew it was only a question of where the renegades would hit. He tried to predict their weakest spot, but he felt they had everything covered. "Easy, Beau, easy," he told his horse.

Riding out of the darkness, like spirits on the wind, the attackers came.

The night riders began firing their Springfields and prepared for the cattle to run. There were fences around the pasture, but Toad knew they couldn't hold against the weight of scared longhorn. Right now it was more important to drive away the invaders than to stem the flow of the cattle.

He had one Indian in the sight of his rifle, when the man suddenly turned and looked squarely at him. Everything began to happen in slow motion.

Toad could plainly see the man had his hair divided into three braids on each side of his head. He saw the feathers. But when he saw the man's face in the starlight, a shiver ran down his body at the hate reflected there.

This was not some unknown person trying to steal the cattle and horses. This man wanted to kill him. And the smoldering hatred made Toad hesitate for a split second. It was long enough for the Indian to fire his rifle first and for Toad to feel the burning in his chest as the bullet sped across the way and through his flesh. The last thing Toad saw was a tiny gleam of satisfaction when the Indian realized Toad was hit and falling from his horse.

It was only then that the full magnitude of the conflict between the settlers and the Indians became plain to Toad. As plain as the face of death. And the last thing Toad said was, "Help me, Lord," as he fell on the hot hide of the long-horn and then bounced underneath the hooves of the moving herd.

After the running battle was over, the men draped Toad's body across his horse and Snake took him back to the ranch house. Daniel came out of the house with his rifle in his hand. "Who is it?" he asked in a tired voice when he saw the body.

"Toad, Captain." Snake saw the sadness on Daniel's face.

"Have the men build a coffin."

At midmorning Daniel, Mary Anna, Tump, Caleb, Mac, Coleman, and Snake gathered at the little cemetery. Mary Anna put a few wildflowers on the three tiny graves of her infants, and then they had the service for Toad.

Daniel read the Twenty-third Psalm and commended the young man to God's keeping. The men covered the coffin with the warm Texas soil, and then Mac placed Toad's saddle over the grave to show anyone who passed by that a good cowboy was buried there. It was the best marker any cowboy could have.

Mary Anna cast one last glance back at the grave. So often she had fought off death for one of her loved ones. The Lord had been merciful to her. She had lost three infants before she had time to get to know them, but so many of the frontier families had lost much, much more.

A chill passed over her as she saw again the three tiny graves. "Sleep well, my babies." She was afraid to say more and left the place of the dead for the place of the living.

❧

One by one the three youngest children came down with a high fever that rapidly advanced to vomiting and runny bowels.

"Daniel," Mary Anna started to say, but he interrupted her.

"I know, take the other children to the Wests' cabin."

Virginia came at once. "The men and older children can take care of things over there. You have your hands full."

Mary Anna used all her tricks to break the fever that sapped life from the children. She tried to get hearty broths down them, but they threw up everything she gave them. She and Virginia literally forced liquids of all kinds down them and even gave them sugar rags to suck.

The nights were the worst. There was little thought of sleep, for while the racking vomiting tore at the women's hearts, they lived in dread of a sudden silence. The specter of three tiny graves doubling the count in the cemetery spurred Mary Anna on, as did her running plea to God to help her and not ask her to give up Oscar, Arthur, and Annah.

"Please, dear Lord," she whispered, "don't take these little ones from me. I can't heal them, but I know Your power can. I knew when I looked down the years with Daniel when we spoke of living out the dream that this was the sort of test we would face. Help us to pass the test and grow stronger from it. But please, dear God, don't take my little ones."

Most of the time she just prayed, "Please, God, please."

One morning Mary Anna woke with terror. She had slept the entire night through without once getting up to check on her children or nurse them. She ran trembling to their little beds.

They were all sleeping peacefully, and she satisfied her fear by lightly running her hand over each cooling forehead. She watched their dear faces as they slept. Annah was only two. Her illness had sapped the baby fat from her little rounded face. It had a pinched look now. The twins, at one, had the same look about them. Where she had seen a fat little cherub in their faces, now she saw thinness. But they were alive and she could build them up again. If only there wasn't some permanent damage done to them that wasn't apparent now. She would have to worry about that later. For now she had them back. She kissed each small forehead and crept over to Virginia's bed.

Virginia awoke with alarm when Mary Anna touched her arm. "No, no, it's all right. Virginia, the fever has broken. They're sleeping!"

"Praise the Lord!" Virginia said, and she immediately got out of bed to look at the children for herself. They hugged each other over the little beds and both began to cry with fatigue and relief.

"We'll have to fatten them up," Virginia said as she wiped

her nose with a handkerchief.

Mary Anna put her arm around Virginia. "We make a good team." Deep gratitude colored her eyes even bluer. "Thank you for being her to help me."

"Oh, pshaw," Virginia said, now wiping her eyes. "You'd do it for me."

"There are very few women on the frontier, and I'm so grateful I'm with someone I love and can share with," said Mary Anna. "You've heard the same stories I have about women going crazy in the loneliness of their cabins with no one to talk with."

Virginia nodded. "I went through a spell of it myself after my little girl died. There was no one there but Caleb, and he nursed his grief in solitude." The sadness went out of her voice. "All the more reason to rejoice right now."

"It seems to me I spend as much time fighting death as I do living. Between the sicknesses and the Indians, it's a full-time job." She sighed. "I tried to explain this to Daniel when we were talking about how good things are for us now that we have the ranch. We aren't going to be protected from life, no matter what. Life itself is a test. And for the Christian it's a test to see if Satan can separate us from God, even in the little things."

"I don't see how any mother can not believe in God," Virginia mused. "Who can look after her children every minute of the day? Who can protect them from the unseen and unknown? Prayer is my peace of mind. I know God'll take care of them, even if I can't."

"But that doesn't mean they won't die," Mary Anna said carefully. "I think that's the thing I'm the most afraid of. I love them when they're born, but now that I know them, I'm not sure I could be as strong as you were, Virginia. I think it would kill me to lose any of my children." She turned away. "It would be the ultimate test. Even harder than losing Daniel. We've had a wonderful life together. I'd miss him more than I can say. But a child hasn't had a chance to find out much of anything. They have so much to live for." She shuddered. "I pray daily that I will never have to go through what you have."

"Let go of the fear, and live life to the fullest. You can't trust God and be afraid everyday. That doesn't make sense, does it?"

"You're right," she said with a slight parting of the lips. "It doesn't make sense."

Oscar began to cry. "Isn't that the loveliest sound?" Virginia hustled over to him. "Come on, little cowboy. Let's try to get some soup into you.

"He's not a cowboy," Mary Anna corrected her. "He's a cattleman." And she smiled, knowing this was the plan, and if God had mercy on them all, Oscar would grow up to be a cattleman like his father.

seven

The spring of 1873 brought the continued recuperations of the three little ones, and the yearly roundup. It seemed to Mary Ann she could set the calendar by the restlessness she felt in Daniel when it was time to get the herd gathered up, counted, and branded. She was reasonably sure he was smart enough not to go on a drive this year and instead send his cattle with the men, as he had done last year. He was hardly old, but the trail was an unforgiving master and made everyone as uncomfortable as possible. There was no such thing as an easy drive.

Daniel and Caleb had their heads together a lot as the summer drew to a close. Mary Anna said nothing, waiting for her level-headed husband to tell her of his plans not to go.

"You're what!" she hissed in the loudest voice she could manage.

Daniel's face wore the look of a man struck by a rattlesnake in own home. "I'm going on the drive with Tump and Peter."

Mary Anna took a deep breath and squared her shoulders. One eyebrow was raised. She pinched her lips together and gritted her teeth. Her face was a mask of anger he hadn't seen since early in their marriage. "You can't be serious," she said in a carefully controlled voice and crossed her arms in front of her.

Defensive now, Daniel stood a little taller. "I am." Then he took a verbal step too near the edge of the abyss. "I'm the boss of this house and this ranch, and if I say I'm going, then by glory, I'm going." His voice thundered through the cabin. He watched Mary Anna's face turn from anger to surprise.

"You've never spoken to me like that before."

"You've never acted like this before. You can't order me around like you do the children. I'm your husband. Head of the house."

She turned her back on him with that remark.

"The drives aren't going to last for very much longer, Mary Anna," he explained reasonably. "A part of history is passing away. There are more fences and people. Soon we'll be hemmed in." He gave a short laugh. "Just like the Indians. I want to make just one more drive myself." Quietly he added, "Maybe I have to prove to myself that at forty I'm not too old to do it."

When she didn't answer, he walked over to her stiff, silent frame and stood behind her. "I won't say any more. If you want to do some more talking about it, I think we'd better do it later. After you've had a chance to think about what I said." He touched her shoulder, but she shrugged him off. Quietly he left the cabin and went out to work with his men.

Mary Anna threw herself on the bed and cried. Then she beat her fist in the covers. After her temper tantrum was over, she sat up and tried to think. *Why did you get so mad?* she asked herself. *He's a cattleman, and this is what cattlemen do. But he doesn't have to. He has more than enough good men to make that drive without him. You're afraid. Of what? That he won't come back. He's always gone so long, and you hate the loneliness. He's choosing to spend time away from you when he doesn't have to. A little boy, still playing cowboy. He should have been over that long ago. What would he do if he stayed here? What he has been doing. Maybe if we start the new house. . .* That thought frightened her, for the Indians were still raiding at will. Word had come that things were worse in Montana and Wyoming. Sitting Bull and Rain-in-the-Face were leading the Plains Indians, and the government was sending more troops to contain the Sioux. That also meant no new troops for Texas.

Mary Anna got up and poured water in the china bowl from the matching pitcher her mother had given her. As she washed her face, she felt herself cooling down, but still angry.

The noise of the children at the supper table covered the silence between husband and wife, but there was no avoiding going to bed together. They were very formal with one another, strangers sharing a bed.

Mary Anna tried hard to get over her anger, but she couldn't let go of it. Daniel left her alone, waiting for his sweet, sensible wife to come back to him.

She was still mad as he prepared to go. "It isn't safe, Daniel. I need you here." The words came out of tight lips.

Quietly he turned from his horse and said, "I'm sorry. But I have to do this. And I'm sorry you don't understand." He leaned down and kissed her still mouth.

She wanted to cry out, "Stay, I love you, I can't bear to see you go, please!" But her lips wouldn't move. She watched him mount up and leave with his men.

She felt as she had when he had gone off to the war. Bereft.

❧

Once on the trail, Daniel began to regret leaving. It was as though Mary Anna had the power to curse the drive. They got off to a late start and everything that could go wrong, did. When at last they got to Dodge, they couldn't find the buyer they had been guaranteed before they started. Jaye Cook and Company Bank in New York closed and caused huge losses of money among the cattlemen.

Daniel sold his cattle for almost what it cost him to take them up there and counted himself lucky that he didn't have to drive them back home. There was no way he could afford to winter them there. It was too costly for the feed and payroll for the men who would agree to do it. He tried to start home early enough for Christmas, but they missed that by weeks.

He thought of Mary Anna every day on the trail. How would things be between them when he got home? She had been right. He shouldn't have gone. It was bitter to have to face her and admit that, after all his bellowing about being the man of the house.

"Papa?" Tump came over to the campfire where they had their bedrolls laid out for the night. Daniel was propped against his saddle, drinking coffee.

"Yes?"

Tump was obviously very uncomfortable about something.

"Sit down, son. Want some coffee?"

"No, thanks."

"Whatever is bothering you can't be that bad. Tell your old papa what's on your mind." Daniel guessed at Tump's age it could be any number of things.

"Do you still love Mama?" Tump looked at Daniel's face to see if he could read the real answer.

Daniel took a deep breath. "Yes, son, I do."

Tump looked down at the fire. "I heard the fight you and Mama had before your left."

Daniel chuckled. "I'm sure half the country heard that fight."

"But you still love her and you're going back to her?"

"With my foot in my mouth and my hat in my hand," Daniel answered. He sighed. "Question is, will she still want me?"

"Of course she does," Tump said quickly. "I mean, what else would she do?"

"Oh, your mama can do pretty well anything she wants to. She's a strong woman. That's why we're still out here. If she wasn't strong, we'd of gone back to Anderson County a long time ago. Or not come at all," he added thoughtfully.

"I know she wants you back," Tump said confidently. "She loves you."

"Maybe. But I sure did a lot to make her not respect me. I said some hard things to her." Daniel took a big swallow of the hot, thick coffee. "She was right, and I was wrong. I shouldn't have come on this drive. Only I was so bound and determined to prove something, I put that first instead of your mama." He looked at his son. "It was a mistake. All I can do is hope she will forgive me and take me back. I've done a lot of damage to the way things are between us. Harsh words are a rocky soil for love to grow in."

"She'll be there, and she'll still love you. I know Mama," Tump said with fervor.

"You can learn a lot from what you heard and saw, boy. Remember not to do it when you're married." Daniel's smile was half-hearted at best.

When they finally rode into the ranch in early January, Mary Anna was not waiting for them on the porch. It was a cold snowy day. The rain clouds looked like a woman dragging her wet gray skirts across the sky, heavy and sodden.

Daniel had bought everyone presents again. He had been especially careful to pick out a fine silver mirror with a matching comb and brush for Mary Anna. He wondered if he'd ever get the chance again to sit behind her rocker on a low stool and brush out her beautiful auburn hair.

❧

When Mary Anna heard the horses come to a stop in front of the cabin, her heart jumped in fear. Daniel must be home. And with him came the next part of their awful fight. She was afraid he didn't love her anymore. Maybe he had only come back to get his things to move into town. She didn't know what to expect. She smoothed her hair, put on a shawl, and opened the door.

Daniel was climbing down off his horse in a slow, old-man fashion. He looked beaten and tired when he turned to face her. His shoulders were slumped, and there was shame on his face.

All her anger melted away and she hurried over to him. He looked very much as he had when he came home from the war.

"You're home," she said carefully, watching his eyes for some sign of affection.

"Yes." He waited to see if he would be accepted or rejected.

"Come inside. I have something warm you can eat."

It was a tiny step forward.

She hugged the boys and gave them plates of food, but they were quiet, waiting to see what would happen. All the other children were asleep. Tump pushed Peter into the other side of the cabin. "Be quiet and eat," he whispered to the questioning look Peter gave him.

Slowly Daniel washed his hands and face, drying them on the towel on the peg by the bowl. Mary Anna turned around to face him as she brought the food.

"Mary Anna! Why didn't you tell me you were going to have a child?" he asked as he saw her enlarged figure.

"I thought you might think I was using it as a weapon to keep you home."

"When?" he asked

"The end of March." She put the food on the table and sat across from him.

He didn't touch the food. "You were right. I shouldn't have gone. It was awful from the first day. You were right." He fought the tears that wanted to spill from his eyes. "And now I'm afraid I've lost you, too."

She reached out her hand toward him. "No, I don't think so." She ducked her head for a moment and then said, "I wasn't sure you would come home to me."

He took her hand and stroked it lightly, carefully. "I did what I had to do, but I shouldn't have done it the way I did. I said some things I'm sorry for. Things that, if you let me stay, you'll never hear again. I promise."

"Then you do want to stay with me?" Her face looked hopeful.

"More than anything in the world. Do you forgive me?"

"Yes, I do. And do you forgive me?"

"Yes, with all my heart." He stood up and walked around to her. She sat still while he caressed her face carefully, then she looked up at him and they kissed softly, tenderly, tentatively. At the far end of the cabin, Tump and Peter quietly slipped up to their beds in the loft.

"I think we'll have to get to know each other all over again," she said.

He grinned. "That will be a pleasure for me. And you will find me a changed man, in many ways."

He helped her up out of the chair. "I'm tired now. I want

to go to bed," she said.

As they slipped between the covers, Daniel stayed carefully on his side of the bed. He wanted to kiss Mary Anna good night, but he wasn't sure if it was the right thing to do.

She slipped her hand into his. He gave it a gentle squeeze. Then he lifted it to his lips and kissed the palm of her hand. Everything was going to be all right now. *Thank You, God. Thank You that I didn't lose her in my stupidity. It was a hard learned lesson. But I won't forget.* Mary Anna still loved him. He was her husband. They would carefully find their way back to one another, but they would try to glue the pieces back on in day-to-day living. Their love wouldn't be the same, but it would be a deeper one, one they had chosen to nurture.

❧

As Daniel settled back into home life, he caught up with the local news. Discovering that Santana and Big Tree had been pardoned and released in October while he was on the trail did nothing to lessen his regret over having gone on the trail. "If they had attacked and I hadn't been here, how would I ever have lived with myself?" he asked.

"They didn't, so no harm was done," Mary Anna reassured him. "Remember what the Bible says, 'Sufficient today is the evil thereof.' We've enough struggles to handle without you borrowing trouble from things that never happened."

When, at the end of January, their baby boy was born dead, Daniel voiced his regrets all over again.

He wept as he held the dead infant in his arms. "It's my fault," he said to Mary Anna. "If I hadn't gone on the drive. . ."

"No, Daniel. It wasn't anyone's fault. It's just life." She gathered Daniel and their little son into the bed with her and they wept together over their loss.

But the seasons of the year can't be stopped, and spring was making a gallant effort to push aside winter. Mary Anna responded to the coming of spring as she always did. She was so finely tuned to its promise, she found healing with the first small green buds. She lavished the love she should have been giving her child on the garden, coaxing each small plant up into the sunlight. And she was able to thank God for the children she did have. She studied them with a new and discerning eye and found new delights.

That summer, both Mary Anna and Daniel were glad to welcome Captain Moorland and his men for a brief visit in the middle of July.

"Congratulations on your promotion, Captain," Daniel said.

"Thank you, but here's what I came out to show you." He was bursting with news. Dramatically he handed Daniel a paper dated earlier that month.

In it, an article described the massacre of Custer at the Little Big Horn by the amassed Sioux. The Indians had been led by Dull Knife, Crazy Horse, Red Cloud, and White Bull. They had wiped out Custer and his men and any chance they had of making peace with the government. They would be hunted down now and eliminated as the enemy. No more peace treaties would be offered.

"They're dead men now," Captain Mooreland said. "And Mackinzie's going after the Comanche up on the Llano Estacado. He'll find them. Every winter they just disappear off the face of the earth. But he'll find them this time." His face was beaming. "We're just about to eliminate our Indian problems."

"And what will happen to the ones who survive?" Mary

Anna asked.

"Reservation. But there won't be that many left, believe me. All the leaders will be caught or killed. Indian territory is where they belong."

His prophecy came true as the year advanced. Mackenzie found the Comanche in Palo Duro Canyon and slaughtered them without mercy. Quannah Parker lasted only until the spring. Starving and ragged, he willingly led the last small band to the reservation. Here and there occasional raids were made, but on a practical level, the Indian nations had been totally defeated.

Erath County, along with the other parts of the country, rejoiced that one of their largest barriers to success had been eliminated. Now they had only the weather, the market, thieves and cutthroats, Texas fever, Kansas farmers, and sodbusters with which to contend.

"Well, Dan," said Caleb. "Now that the danger is over, I think we should both get on with the next part of the plan. I'll be moving Virginia into town as soon as I can build us a house there."

"We're going to miss you something awful." Daniel smiled. "We're getting ready to build that mansion I want for Mary Anna."

Caleb shook his head. "I don't know how we did it, but we did. I have everything I've ever wanted."

"You do, too, know how we did it. God has blessed us at every turn. Even the bad ones," Daniel added with chagrin.

Daniel and Mary Anna turned their attention to building their new home. They had chosen a design from an architectural plan book, and Daniel quickly ordered the materials out of Waco, Texas.

The Victorian style house had two stories with a huge porch

wrapped around it like loving arms. Its gingerbread trim would be painted dark brown, but the house itself would be dark green. Spacious closets and two bathrooms, an almost unheard of luxury, were among its finest features.

The men at the Berlin Lodge in Stephenville razzed Daniel endlessly about the bathrooms, but it was in good humor. Before the house was finished, almost every man in the lodge had an opportunity to use his special skills to make the house one of beauty and everyone's pride.

"There is one thing I want," Daniel told the men. "I need running water for the house. I need someone to find it. Know of anyone who can find water?"

"I can take care of that," said Joe.

The new house was in its last building stages when an old woman as thin and willowy as the forked branch she brought with her came to the ranch with her husband. Her smile was big as she told him, "There's a lots of shallow pools of water around here. Secret rivers run just beneath the ground and meet up with other rivers." She took the peach branch in her hand, a fork in each one and held the branch level as she began walking. She walked around the front of the house, concentrating on the end of the limb. "No," she shook her head. "Nothing here." She walked to the side of the house.

Daniel was watching the end of the limb carefully, too. He thought he saw it twitch. The woman's skirts swished as she walked through the tall grass. The stick seemed to be pulling her along, and as she got several yards from the house, the end of the stick suddenly dipped toward the ground. The woman stopped still. "Here. Here is where the water is. It's down about fifty feet, but it's here."

Daniel was astonished at the procedure, but he marked the place she indicated. She held out her hand for the money she was to be paid. "When it comes in, I'll come back for the other half of my money." She smiled a toothy grin and climbed up in the wagon with the help of her husband.

"I admit I have some reservations about all this, but you're a mighty impressive woman," Daniel told her.

"It's a gift, Mr. Thornton. I claim no praise and want no shame from it. I use it as best I can."

Several days later the driller came out to dig the well. Mary Anna heard the heavy rattling of his wagons.

He stopped in front of the cabin. "Hello, the house!" he shouted.

When Daniel appeared, the wizened black man scrambled nimbly down from the tall seat. He had an equally thin, dark-skinned boy with him. The old man stuck out his dirty hand.

"Manilla's my name and water's my game. This here is Mandan. Indian kid. Onliest word he would say when I first found him. Name of his tribe, I think. So you want water, do you?"

"Yes, for the new house over there."

They walked over to the work in progress. "Gonna be a big, beautiful house, Mr. Thornton. Mandan is the onliest person alive who can really find water. Never fails. He's the son of a real Indian medicine man."

Daniel looked at the teenager boy who was dressed in ragged castoffs. His hair was matted, and he looked any-thing but the son of a shaman.

"Cost you a dollar fer him to find it."

Daniel didn't tell the man about the water woman. "That'll be just fine."

"Earn yer keep, boy. Find us some water," the man or-dered. The boy moved with grace and ease, striding the front ground of the house. He frowned and retraced his steps to the far side of the house and then moved to the back. He made his way around the house to the side in the general area the water woman had chosen, walking slowly in a careful pattern designed to cover the whole ground. He paused, cocked his ear toward the earth. Then he walked to the exact spot where the water woman had pointed. "Here," is all he said.

"Git the wagon lined up, Mandan. How far down?"

Mandan extended all five fingers of one hand.

"Right at fifty feet," Manila nodded confidently.

Mandan removed the back wheels which placed the heavy machinery on the ground. The derrick was raised and the cable spool set. Like a carefully choreographed ballet, Manilla and Mandan pulled the heavy rope off the cable spoon, through the crown and spudding.

Mandan unhitched the mules and secured the pale yellow rope. As they patiently walked their endless circle, they would provide power to turn the machine that would raise and lower the ponderous stem. That in turn pounded the heavy fourteen-inch bit into the ground.

The bit yo-yoed in the ever-deepening hole as the earth it dug was moved to the top. Drilling was hard, dirty work and it took skillful knowledge to keep the bit chewing at the earth.

"There it is! Fifty-one feet exactly. Tolt ya so!" The water licked at the mud-encrusted bottoms of Manila's pants, then slowly ebbed out of sight.

Manilla and Mandan had captured the attention of everyone on the ranch, and when the water was found, a shout went up from the crowd. Mandan stopped down, cautiously opened a small leather pouch, and dropped in a pinch of damp earth from the new well.

"All right men, get the pieces of that big Standard windmill and get it set up," said Daniel. They erected the elevated redwood tank and ran the pipes into the house. A simple opening of a valve brought water from the tank. It was a proud moment when Mary Anna opened it and water flowed from the spout. "It's a miracle, Daniel. It's a miracle," she breathed as the water cascaded over her hand.

Daniel went back outside to tell Manilla the job was complete and to pay him. "Best sixty-six dollars I ever spent!" he said as he paid the man.

Manila handed one of the dollars to Mandan, who climbed up on the wagon seat and sat impassively. Then Manilla joined him and urged his mules on to the next job.

Daniel went into the house. In the kitchen he could hear the groanings of the big blades as they turned in the hot prairie wind. The sound would become a constant companion to the house.

Now that there was water, the work on the house progressed at a rapid rate. The furniture Daniel ordered from Waco came, and soon he and Mary Anna were standing in their dream home.

Daniel was especially proud of the huge claw-footed tubs. It was almost the first thing he showed everyone who came to see their new home. At night, carbide lights gave the house a warm glow. The house was built up on a high rock foundation that helped keep it cool in the summer. Thick rugs on the floor would keep it warm in the winter. The house seemed to have everything.

"I've never seen anything like it," said Mac in a voice of awe as he entered the new dwelling. His hat was in his hand, and he was followed by the other cowboys as Daniel gave them the grand tour.

When Virginia and Caleb came for a call, Mary Anna was proud to show them her new home. Caleb and Daniel were a little embarrassed at the girlish joy with which Mary Anna and Virginia met one another. It reminded Daniel of two little schoolgirls who hadn't seen each other in a while. He motioned for Caleb to come into the big parlor on the right side of the house.

"Ah, Daniel, don't be so hard on 'em. They haven't seen each other since we moved to town," Caleb grinned. He looked around the room. "Son, I think you're living in a castle." He sat down in one of the deep leather chairs and crossed his legs.

"Yes, I think I am." He offered Caleb something to drink and said, "You know, you're one of the few people who can truly understand what the culmination of this house means to me."

"It's true. Now our house may not be quite this grand, but it's everything I ever wanted—'cepting I only have one bathroom," he smiled and raised one eyebrow. "And unless I'm mistaken, it looks like you're getting ready to add another child to your family pretty soon. Son, you're doing all right. I don't know if you kin stand another good piece of news."

Daniel was sitting in the matching chair next to him. "News?"

"Yes. The men in the lodge think it's time for you to run again for county commissioner. We think you're a shoo-in."

Daniel flushed and then sputtered, "I'd love to run again. I know this time how to run a campaign a little better than that first time."

"And we plan to hep you."

They raised their glasses, and Caleb said, "To the new county commissioner."

Virginia and Mary Anna were in the master bedroom,

sitting on a beautiful sofa in the sitting area, having their refreshments.

Virginia's merry eyes twinkled. "And so when is the new baby due?"

"September. I'm somewhat embarrassed to be having babies still at my age."

"Well, it gets more dangerous, but you can't ignore what the Lord sends. I'll help you when you're time comes."

"And you. How is living in town?"

"Glorious. I love every minute of it." Her glance took in the beautiful room. "You could talk me into living out here with you anytime, though," she grinned. "You have it all, Mary Anna. A husband who loves you, a good family, a beautiful home. What more could there be?"

Mary Anna's big smile faded a bit. "I do have it all. And I'm grateful to God for everything you mentioned. But sometimes I get scared, wondering if I'm supposed to have it all." She looked at her teacup. "Or what price I have to pay for it."

"Don't be silly. God blesses the people He wants without them having to pay a price for it. A blessing is that. A blessing."

"I guess I don't feel like I deserve all this," Mary Anna said truthfully.

"No one does. But we enjoy it all the same without looking over our shoulder for something bad to happen."

"You're still a comfort to me, Virginia. Let's see each other often."

"Let's."

It wasn't long until Virginia made a very hurried trip out to the house again.

Mary Anna was lying at the foot of the big bed in a little labor bed. In between contractions she tried to rest. "I'm getting too old for this, Virginia," she repeated.

"Well, you know what to do about it. Here, push. Push!"

Mary Anna was remembering the four babies who had not cried when she had delivered them or whose cry had been silenced too soon. *Please, God, let this one be all right.*

The sound Mary Anna waited for came quickly. The red-faced infant squalled indignantly at his new world, and Mary Anna laughed out loud at the healthy sound of it. Virginia could barely wait to call Daniel in.

He knelt at the edge of the small bed beside Mary Anna, who was holding the baby. "I want you two to meet properly. Daniel, this is Little Dan. Little Dan, meet your wonderful father."

"Little Dan?"

"I don't want anyone calling him Junior, though his name will be Daniel Robert Thornton, the second."

And more blessings were added. Daniel was elected county commissioner in the 1876 elections. At the lodge meeting, he said, "I'm donating two and a half acres of land for the Barton Springs school." Grinning, he added, "I'm not doing this because I'm so noble. I'm doing it because my wife has hounded me to death for a real school building."

The men laughed heartily, and Mr. Trent said, "You know that means a new building for us, too. First floor is the school. Second floor is the meeting place for the lodge." All the men cheered and clapped.

Daniel was feeling very good when he entered his warm new home. But Mary Anna was crying up in their bedroom.

"What in the world?" he said in alarm and ran to where she was lying in the bed, awash in tears.

"I'm pregnant again!" And she dissolved in more tears. "I'll never get to go anywhere for the rest of my life or entertain in our big lovely house. I'll be in seclusion forever."

Daniel was no fool. He was tickled to death, but he knew

better than to say that to his wife. She needed comforting. "I think this thing about seclusion is silly. Everybody knows where babies come from. Why shouldn't you be allowed to go where you please? At least for a long while."

She sat up and looked at him in disbelief. "Do you really think so?"

"Yes, I do. I'm proud you're going to have our child. There's no need to hide the fact that a married woman is going to give birth." He hoped he sounded convincing.

"You know, you're right. I haven't done anything wrong. I'm married. I'm not going to hide away. At least not at the beginning. Let's have a party and invite everyone!"

The town responded pretty well as a whole. The older women seem to be the most sympathetic. They had been through it. The younger women were thankful that someone was breaking a rule they thought was silly.

So when Minnie Kathleen, whom they nicknamed Kate, was born, the town accepted her as a move toward a more modern society.

Daniel and Mary Anna celebrated their twenty-fifth wedding anniversary that summer, and Daniel gave her the last part of his promise: perfectly matched diamond earrings. She cried and cried and protested she didn't need anything else, but she wore them from that day until the day she died.

Life was so sweet, sometimes Mary Anna thought she was living in a dream. She knew that somewhere down the line bad things could still happen. They were not immune to hardship and sorrow. But now were days filled with love and joy.

The joy dimmed when she delivered a still-born girl, but she knew in her heart there would never be another child. She gloried in the ones she had and loved them with all her heart.

eight

1886

Daniel looked at the sky again. The early morning promised no clouds on the horizon. He and his neighbors needed the rain badly. He had a big store of grain, but the crops in his fields were burning up just like everyone else's.

He wiped his brow and the inside of his hat with his big handkerchief and said to Mary Anna who was sitting on the porch snapping beans, "We'll still make a profit this year, no need to worry."

"I wasn't worrying. You have those new horses you had sent from England. The mares are about ready to foal. The sale of those horses alone would see us through."

He came up to the porch and sat down on the bottom step. He could smell the greenness of the beans as she snapped them open and pulled down the string to discard.

"Talked to Charlie. Have you seen the paper?"

"No. Something I need to know?"

"Oh, I was feeling a little blue when I read about Santana."

"What about Santana?"

"He threw himself out of the window at the Texas State Prison. He's dead."

"Let me see the article."

Daniel got the paper from inside and she scanned the news about their old enemy. It called him "The Orator of the Plains." It quoted much of his 1867 Medicine Lodge speech about how much he loved to roam over the prairies and he didn't want to settle on the reservation. The speech ended with the words, "I see the white man cut down my timber, kill my buffalo, and when I see that my heart feels like bursting."

Once again terrible guilt filled Mary Anna's heart. They had taken the land, spoiled it for the Indians, and driven an entire nation of people out of their homes onto a confined area. Tears formed in her eyes as she thought of the many desperate battles she had fought against this man and others to make her home in Erath County. They were both right and wrong for what they had done to the Indians. Surely it could have been handled in a different way. How did it come to this?

"This made you sad?" she asked Daniel.

"Yes. I guess somewhere it will be written that the white man was the good guy and the Indian was the bad guy. If the truth is ever told, it will say there was good and bad on both sides. I needed land to make a living after the war. This was my best chance. It was a lot of people's best chance. When we came out here, we thought the Indian tribes would share with us. We had no idea what chain of events we were setting off." He sighed deeply. "I'm sorry it ended the way it did. But I'm not sorry I came out here and defended my right to own the land and improve it. Just look at what we provide for ourselves and others. Horses, cattle, wheat, cotton, peaches. We have done good things for the community, too. Gave that land for the school." He paused and looked up at Mary Anna.

"Who are you trying to convince?" she smiled.

"Me, of course." His grin was a little crooked. "I wonder what our children will have to conquer to have their dreams come true?"

"I'm sure something will turn up."

"I want it to, so they'll be strong and noble and honorable."

"I'm afraid I don't believe some of the things that were done were so honorable," she said carefully.

Daniel's face darkened. "Years ago when your father and I led that raid on the reservation, we thought we were doing the right thing. The jury must have thought so, too."

"No, they didn't think your were right. They said you were wrong, but they didn't want you punished because of all the Indian raids and killing. They hoped the raid you all made on the reservation would stop the Indians, though."

"They were wrong. But I can't see there was any other way to stay alive out here but the way we did it."

"No point in trying to relive and change the past. It's over." She took her pan from her lap and headed for the door. "Do you want me to bring you some lemonade?"

"Please." He wiped his face again. His white shirt was sticking to his body like a wet sheet. He listened to the sound of the windmill, turning slowly in the light breeze, and smiled at the predictable noise it made. It was as comforting as a mother's lullaby. In the house he could hear Mary Anna talking to Elizabeth through the open windows. The lace curtains fluttered in and out as the wind ebbed and flowed through the house. He was a content man. Well, almost content. He still worried about the rain. He would be all right, but many of his neighbors wouldn't be if they didn't get the rain in the next few days. "Lord, we sure could use some of Your cooling waters on our thirsty crops," he prayed.

Two riders came toward the house, and Daniel soon recognized them as his sons Willie and Henry. They tethered their horses in the shade of the trees.

"Is Mama around?" Willie asked.

"No, she's in the house."

"Good," said Henry. They sat down on either side of their father.

"What am I getting hit up for this time? More money?" he asked suspiciously.

"No, something more important." Henry got closer to his father and dropped his voice down low. "Willie and I want to go back to Anderson County instead of going back to the Huckabee Academy this fall." His twenty-year-old eyes were dark blue and filled with a longing for adventure.

"Anderson!" Daniel exclaimed quietly. "What in the world for?"

"The same reason you came out here. Adventure. We want to seek our fortunes," Willie said dramatically.

"Your fortune is right here on this ranch, and you know it. You may want some adventure, but don't try to sell me a wind-broke horse," Daniel said huffily.

Henry tried a different tack. "You found your true love back there in Tennessee Colony. Why can't we go back there and maybe find ours?"

Daniel grinned broadly. "You two have been thinking on this a long time, haven't you?"

"Yes, sir, we have," said Henry. "But you know how Mama is about schooling. You'd have to be the one to ask her if we could go."

"You know her answer will be no," Daniel stated flatly.

"That's why we want you to ask her. You have a way of saying things to her to make her listen," added Willie earnestly.

Daniel laughed out loud at that statement. "I did try once to make her listen," he said thinking of the failed trail drive many years before. "I promised myself I'd never do that again. Nearly cost me my marriage," he said under his breath. "No. I can't make her listen." He looked at the boys' fallen faces. "But if I can work it into the conversation at the right time,

I'll approach her about it. It's a good thing you boys started early on this project. It may take a long while to get a yes out of your mama."

Just then the screen door opened and Mary Anna appeared with a tray of lemonade and glasses. "I thought I heard you boys out here with your father. You look real serious. Is anything wrong?"

"No, ma'am," they chorused.

"We were just talking about the weather. About how we need the rain," Henry added.

"You looked pretty worried about it from inside the house," she said as she handed out the cold glasses of pale yellow lemonade.

"Believe me, it's something to worry about," Daniel said casually.

The boys drank their lemonade quickly and made excuses to leave.

Their feet had barely left the porch when Mary Anna said, "And what did those two want? It must be something pretty big for them to come to you behind my back." Her eyes narrowed as she tried to guess what they were up to.

"Oh, you know boys," Daniel said noncommittally.

"I know those two. Now what did they want?"

Daniel grinned. "You don't give up, do you?"

"That's how I got you,"

He joined in her teasing laughter. "I believe it was the other way around. Funny how your memory fails you when you want it to," he smiled.

"And?" she persisted

"They want to go back to Tennessee Colony."

"Well, I never would have guessed that one," said Mary Anna calmly. "What for?"

"Well, first it was to seek their fortunes, then it was adventure, and lastly it was to look for a wife because that's where I found you and you're the best there is, so there surely should be some fine young women for them."

"Hmm."

He watched her in surprise. "I thought you'd be mad."

"Oh, all the women's magazines advise that women keep their men guessing in order to keep their marriages from getting boring. I don't want to be predictable all the time," she said sweetly. Too sweetly.

"You're mad," he said.

"Not exactly mad. But puzzled. Whatever gave them the idea to go back to our roots? They've heard a lot of stories of us living there, but I didn't think those old tales would inspire the boys to want to go back. We probably don't have anyone there who even remembers us."

Daniel's eyes sparkled wickedly. "Maybe Amos Strong is still there preaching."

Mary Anna colored slightly. "I haven't thought of him in years and years. He wouldn't remember me even if he were there," she insisted.

"I think he would," Daniel said. "I don't think he'll ever forget you."

"Now, Daniel, you know there was never anything between Amos Strong and me!"

"Don't get your Irish up. I know there wasn't anything from your side. But I am certain if I hadn't come back from the war, he would have asked you to marry him. And I think you would have done it. He was a fine man." He paused a moment and added impishly, "How long were you prepared to wait for me?"

"About one more day," she said teasingly. "Good thing you made it." She turned serious. "When do the boys want to go, and how long do they plan to stay?"

"I don't think they got that far with the plan yet. The first move was to get around you."

"Let me think about it. Don't tell them I know yet."

"I didn't say I was letting them go. I said I wanted to think about it."

That night at supper Mary Anna watched the two boys covertly. They were handsome in different ways. Henry was tall and broad-shouldered like his father. He had Daniel's coloring, too. Willie was more like her. His hair was dark auburn like hers, but he had grey eyes and sprinkles of freckles along the bridge of his patrician nose. *How did they grow up to be men in such a short while? I can't bear the thought of them going off so far, but if I don't let them, how can they grow like we did? I know some of the girls are sweet on these two. They're too handsome not to have somebody flirting with them. I'll speak to Elizabeth about it right away. Surely there is someone in town for them.*

After supper, Mary Anna broached the subject with her daughter while they did the dishes.

"Why, yes, all four of the older boys have at least a couple girls with crushes on them. In fact, I'd say they were pretty much the catch of the day around Stephenville. Why?"

When Mary Anna explained about the boys' trip, Elizabeth said, "Looks like it's time to have some parties around here if you want to keep them home. Matchmaking time," she grinned. "You'll have to make up your mind, Mama, if you're going to chose the wives for your seven sons or if you're going to let it happen. Kate, Annah, and I will chose our own, thank you."

"Tump is already in love with Molly, and Peter is stuck on Parcinda. Arthur and Oscar and Little Dan are too young to worry about yet. It's just Henry and Willie I need to worry about right now." She turned and looked at Elizabeth. "And you? Is Henry C. Wylie coming to call for your hand any time soon?"

"Mama! How do you know all these things?"

"I can read minds. All mothers can. It comes to you when you hold your first baby in your arms. It sure saves a lot of time," she grinned. Then she looked serious. "The house will seem very empty without you, and I know it won't be long before you become a bride. I think Henry Wylie is a fine man. He'll take good care of you."

Elizabeth looked in her mother's steady eyes. "Thank you, Mama. I love him very much. We plan to stay right here in Erath County."

"I'll bet your father might have a little land for your dowry that won't be too far away," she smiled.

That night, as they often did, Mary Anna and Daniel talked long into the early hours of the morning. By dawn, the unsuspecting boys were given their chance for adventure with their mother's blessing. Henry and Willie were stunned by the news.

"I don't have to tell you the most important thing is for you to get there and back safely," Daniel warned. "And you must be back by Thanksgiving."

A few days later Mary Anna hugged each one in turn. "I'm leaving your safety in God's hands, but don't do anything stupid to tempt Him." She was sober and dry eyed as they climbed into their saddles with a map of Texas to guide them.

The dazed young men were suddenly on their way, and wild with the joy and anticipation of such a dream coming true. They carried their mother's letter to Amos Strong, if he was still there, asking him to watch over her boys.

The trip itself turned out not to be very exciting. But when they got to Tennessee Colony, they immediately stopped by the hotel their grandfather had once owned and where their mother had cooked.

"Oh, yes, I remember the Garland family," said the present owner. "Good people," he added. And yes, Reverend Strong could be found down at the church he pointed out.

When Amos answered the door, Henry said, "Sir, we're Henry and Willie Thornton, Mary Anna and Daniel's boys. Our folks wanted us to look you up if you were still here."

Amos was so surprised to see them, he almost forgot to invite them in. "I think I would have known you two. You're both very like your parents." He offered them food while he read Mary Anna's letter. He chuckled in a few places. It was a friendly letter, and the last part asked him to keep a watchful eye on her boys. He took on that task gladly, for the reason he had never remarried was his love for Mary Anna. He had never found anyone quite like her.

The boys went to church on Sunday. It was the proper way to meet girls. and it wasn't long until the boys met the Kenny girls. From the moment Henry met Florence Bell Kenny, he was a lost soul. He beheld her as the embodiment of everything feminine of which he had dreamed. Her saucy ways and ready wit drew him like the proverbial moth to the flame. In all his twenty long years of living, no one had ever smitten him the way she did.

She had a younger sister named Jackie, and Willie felt she was the jewel in the queen's crown. Something funny happened to his stomach every time she smiled at him, which was frequently. In many ways she was more beautiful than her older sister, and Willie couldn't believe she thought him more than a country bumpkin. Words seem to cleave to the roof of his mouth every time he tried to say something clever to her. He was sure she thought him a perfect donkey. The two young men were granted permission to call on the young ladies. They were terrified.

"Do you think her father likes us?" Willie worried.

"We come from a good family that's well-known." Henry replied.

"I hope they're well-known in this part of the country, too." Willie looked up into the heavens. "Oh, thank you, Mama, that you made us go to school and learn to be gentlemen."

"That's a big plus, all right," agreed Henry. "A lot of good it does me, though. Half the time around her, I bump into furniture and spill my cup of tea in the saucer," he said sadly.

"I didn't think that being in love could make me feel so, so, awkward," sighed Willie.

"I've always felt real slick around girls. Cocky. But when I look into Miss Florence's eyes, I turned into a cow-eyed dope."

They presented themselves to the Kenny home at precisely three o'clock. They followed the prescribed rituals of courtship, careful never to do anything that would offend the young ladies or their parents, who were always in attendance.

After they had spent countless agonizing hours of small talk and short walks, Henry and Willie decided to ask for the girls' hands in marriage at the same time. Both were total wrecks as the hour of their meeting with Mr. Kenny approached.

"I can't say this comes as a surprise to us," Mr. Kenny assured them. "However, we were surprised at the quickness of your offers of marriage."

Mr. Kenny helped himself to a careful bite of oatmeal cookie. Both young men refused his offer, for they knew they would never be able to get the cookies down their constricted throats. They tried to read his actions or his face for some sort of hint as to what his answer would be. Henry decided in his mind that Mr. Kenny would make one great poker player, for nothing was visible on his chubby face. He crossed his legs and looked at them. "Mr. Thornton," he said to Willie, "my wife and I feel Miss Jackie is much too young to even consider a marriage proposal at this time. And to take her away to Erath County, well, I'm sure you can appreciate our position."

Willie felt the ground fall away from his feet.

"And as for your request, Mr. Thornton," he said to Henry, "we feel you are perhaps, shall we say, a little too happy-go-lucky in your attitude toward life." His eyebrows rose with his statement.

The words cascaded over Henry like scalding tea. Happy-go-lucky! Those certainly were not words he attached to himself. But the words were hanging like a sword over his dream of marriage and it neatly severed it.

"But, sir," Henry tried to say.

"We are of course flattered you should want to join our family."

"And our family would be overjoyed at having these two wonderful young women join ours," Henry said a little heatedly at the implication. "Our father and mother are prominent citizens of Stephenville. You can ask Reverend Strong."

"Yes, yes, I'm sure they're important in their own little town. However," he rose, leading the way to the door, "our final answer is no. Thank you for coming."

The boys were standing in a daze on the front porch with the door being firmly shut in their faces.

As they walked silently back to the hotel, Amos intercepted them. "You two look like you've been ridden hard and put away wet." And then he remembered their errand. "Oh," he said carefully. "You've been to see Mr. Kenny." He steered the boys to his home.

"I should have told you this before, but I've seen the way Miss Florence and Miss Jackie look at you. I thought maybe you'd have a chance. Many men have courted them, and all have been rejected out of hand. It isn't you. Mr. Kenny won't let them go until he finds rich men for them."

"We aren't exactly poor," Henry said.

"But they love us, I know they do!" Willie said desperately.

"If they love you, and you love them, then I say you should press your suit with Mr. Kenny. Don't give up. And don't let him get you down." He stood in front of them. "Are you willing to fight for your true loves?"

"Yes," said Henry, nearly in tears.

"Yes," added Willie heartily.

"Get jobs. Stay here. Go to every church social. Even if you're not their escorts, you must take every opportunity to be with them. Let Mr. Kenny see how much you care." It was good advice and they followed it.

Finally Henry could stand it no longer. He and Willie decided to ask the two young women to elope with them.

"Miss Jackie won't do it, I'm sure," Willie said sadly.

But Henry was hopeful. He got his chance at a social at the church. He and Florence were sitting at the edge of the gazebo, listening to the laughter coming from the river where boaters were lazing down the ebony water.

"I have to talk to you. You haunt my dreams every night. All I think of the whole day is you." The sharp intake of her breath made him hope she felt the same way, too. He pushed on. "Do you miss me?"

She dropped her gaze so that her lashes feathered against her soft cheeks. "Of course I miss you. We've had such fun together."

"You know what I mean. Miss Florence, I love you and I want to marry you," he said recklessly.

"Hush! Do you want someone to hear you?" But the words weren't angry. He took heart.

"Do you love me?" His eyes were wide with hope.

Once again she avoided his direct look. "Yes," she said softly, "I do. But there is nothing to be done about it now."

"I'll wait forever," he promised. His heart was pounding in a counterpoint to the waltz coming from the community building. *She said she loves me,* it beat out crazily.

"They'll never let us marry," she said miserably.

"If you could, would you marry me?" His whole future rested on the next few words, and he held his breath in order to hear each one clearly.

"Yes." She looked into his eyes. "Yes, I would."

Henry took a deep breath to steady himself. "Would you elope with me?"

"Why, Henry, that's the most romantic thing I ever heard of! Yes, yes, yes!" Her eyes gleamed with excitement.

"Tomorrow night. Reverend Strong will marry us. Oh, Florence, I love you with all my heart."

"Henry, you're the most romantic man I've ever met. I'll arrange to stay with a friend tomorrow night. Then I'll wear a red bonnet and hide in the bushes at the edge of town. I'll leave Mama and Papa a note so they won't worry."

Willie's face showed the desperation and the despair at the answer Miss Jackie gave him. "I'm going to die without her," he told his brother.

Amos could see the love in Henry's eyes, but he was against an elopement.

"If you won't marry us, we'll elope and we'll get married on the way," Henry said firmly. He looked at Amos with big eyes, "I'd rather you be the one to marry us."

Amos caved in. "Somehow or another I'm sure to get blamed for this whole thing," Amos said. "My hide won't be worth a nickel when Kenny gets through with me. I may as well go with you. I never thought I'd get caught up in a triangle like this."

Amos told everyone he was going back with the Thorntons, and the Kennys sighed in relief that the young men had given up their foolish suits.

Amos's wagon was packed in the daylight where everyone could see it. At the edge of town that night, Henry nervously scanned the bushes. At last he spotted the bright red bonnet and the lovers were reunited. Amos wouldn't stop until they were far away.

Their church was an arbor of trees beside a glittering stream. Florence carried wildflowers and wore her big red bonnet. Willie served as best man and father of the bride. The birds sang in notes almost too sweet for human ears. Amos read their vows, and Henry claimed his bride.

"I'll buy you the prettiest ring I can when we get home," Henry promised.

"The ring doesn't matter," Florence whispered. "My heart is wed to yours, ring or no ring," and she offered her lips for him to kiss again.

The four hurried to the wagon and continued their trip to the safety of Barton Springs.

While the newlyweds talked softly to one another in the back of the wagon, Willie talked with Amos for comfort. Willie poured out his broken heart to him.

"If you love her that much, don't give up on marrying her. Jacob had to marry Leah before he was able to win Rachel. And that took seven years."

That didn't comfort Willie much. "I can't wait that long."

As they neared the ranch, Willie took his horse and rode on ahead.

Mary Ann wrapped her arms around his neck and almost choked him with her joy. "Where's Henry?" Alarm in her voice hurried Willie to tell the story of the elopement.

"Eloped! Her parents didn't approve?" The very idea that someone wouldn't approve of one of her children sparked Mary Anna's Irish temper to the fullest. But she was happy if Henry was. "Married a Tennessee Colony girl. Daniel, did you hear that? He's bringing back a bride." Mary Anna saw the pain in Willie's eyes. "And you?"

"I found her, but her parents said she's too young to marry, and I couldn't convince her to elope with me."

"I'm sorry, son," Daniel said.

And then the happy couple, with Amos driving, came in view.

Mary Anna gave the nervous bride a warm hug. "Welcome home, child," she said. "You're Henry's wife, and we love you already for that. I'm sure we'll love you even more as we get to know you better."

Florence cried in Mary Anna's arms. "Thank you. I was so afraid, well, you know."

"I do think you should write your folks a letter. You owe that to them."

"I left a note with my friend."

"Nevertheless, you write." Mary Anna's voice was motherly. "Now let me hug this fine man standing next to you. Henry, you did well, She's lovely."

Then she walked to Amos and silently enfolded him in a warm embrace. "Hello, Amos. It's a joy to see you again. You look well. You must have traded reading your Bible for Romeo and Juliet."

He grinned broadly. "Your son is hard to say no to. A real Thornton." He walked over to Daniel. "Hello, old friend. Your boys have told me of your successes. They're very proud of you."

Daniel pulled him into a warm bear hug. "Thank you, Amos. Looks like you've taken care of my family once again.

Let's go in and celebrate!"

Amos said with admiration, "I don't think I've ever been in a house this grand."

"It's home," Mary Anna said. They sat in the more relaxed atmosphere of the second parlor, and Mary Anna served refreshments. "Are you here to stay?" she asked Amos.

"It appears that I'm a fugitive. I sure can't go back to Tennessee Colony."

Mary Anna smiled. "We need a minister for our church. The circuit rider doesn't get here often enough for most of us.

Daniel cleared his throat officially. "I happen to be on the pulpit committee. I think I can guarantee you a job, Amos." He looked levelly at Amos. "I'm glad you're here. And you're welcome in our home anytime."

Later that night up in their bedroom, Mary Anna was pondering over all the events of the day. She thought it a shame that a nice man like Amos had never remarried. He'd make such a good husband and father. *Maybe he'll find his love here in Stephenville.* The thought made her happy.

"What are you thinking about?" Daniel asked. "You look sad and happy at the same time."

A slight blush highlighted her cheeks. "I was thinking about Amos," she admitted. "I was wondering why he never married again after his wife and children were killed by the Comanches. That was so many years ago."

Daniel came to her and took her in his arms, looking deeply into her eyes. "I think we both know the reason." He kissed her. "It's because I was the lucky one."

She nestled against him. "I love you, Daniel."

"I know." And he placed his lips softly against hers again.

nine

Fall began to sprinkle a few colors about the trees, changing greens into violent reds, deep purples, and flaming oranges. The nights became cool again and everyone slept better.

Daniel went into town for his monthly lodge meeting. Mary Anna went with him, and he dropped her off at the white planked church for her weekly quilting.

She enjoyed the company, and made quick, neat little stitches as she joined the lively conversation. It was a relaxing time of harmless gossip, recipe and remedy exchanges, and good natured complaining. They were working on a Texas Star quilt.

In the course of the morning's news, Annie Frank happily announced, "I planted flowers around the back of the church today."

"Well, they won't be there tomorrow," said gray-haired Gertrude Jones. "The way the town lets the pigs run around loose is a crime. As soon as they find those flowers, they'll root them right up." Her lips were set in a firm angry line.

"She's right," piped a small birdlike woman, appropriately named Dovie. "I've planted flowers before, and that's exactly what happened. What we need is a fence to keep the pigs out."

"What we need is to keep the pigs in the pens where they should be," Gertrude said sharply.

"That'll be the day," mocked a stout lady with a florid face. "If that ever happens, I'd think civilization had finally come to Stephenville."

"Then why don't we just put up the fence?" Mary Anna asked reasonably.

"We still don't have the money to put up a fence," said Gertrude tartly, "or we would have done it a long time ago." There was rebuke at Mary Anna's stupidity in her voice, but Mary Anna was not offended. Gertrude was known for her pessimistic view of life, and Mary Anna often wondered what had happened to give her such a sour disposition and the will to express it at every opportunity.

"We could sell quilts and have bake sales to raise money, I suppose," said Dovie.

"We'd be the ones to buy the quilts and baked goods," said Gertrude. "Might as well just dig up the money out of our own pockets."

"Morning, ladies," a cheerful voice called out. It was Gertrude's husband, come to fetch her.

Mary Anna was glad to see him, for a small pinch of Gertrude's outlook on life went a long way.

"We were just talking about you men," his wife said in a complaining voice.

"I'll just bet you were, my dear," he said amiably.

How has he lived with her all these years and stayed so happy? Mary Anna wondered.

"We're going to raise money to build a fence to keep out the pigs so we can have flowers to beautify the church," said stout Pearl Harrison.

The women all looked at Gertrude to see if she would allow Pearl to overrule her assessment of how to get the money.

Gertrude's husband, Walter, was a rotund man, and he stood there with his hat in his hand, stroking his walrus mustache. He was dressed as a prosperous man, and always gave the appearance of good humor. "I'll tell you what, ladies. I know all about what goes on at these quilting meetings. I'll give you fifty dollars for your fence." He smiled beatifically.

"What!" they chorused.

"If," he said smiling broadly and confidently, "you women can sit here for the whole day and quilt without saying so much as one word."

Heads swivelled from one lady to another. "Well, I never," began one lady.

"Wait," said Pearl to Mr. Jones. "I think that's a wonderful idea. We'll take you up on your most generous offer," she said graciously inclining her head toward him.

"But. . . ," began the nervous Dovie.

"Thank you for getting us a fence built," said Pearl. She winked at the ladies around the quilting frame.

Mr. Jones was a bit taken back by her confidence. "I'll send my freedman over to sit with you next week," he said. "We surely want to do this fairly," he added with a smile.

Mary Anna could tell by his attitude that he felt sure his offer was safe.

On the appointed day, Mr. Jones came by the church with his freedman and entered the room where the women were already busily working. He burst into loud, raucous laughter. He laughed so hard, tears rolled down his ample cheeks. The ladies were sitting around the frame, quilting steadily. Each one had a gag tied firmly over her mouth.

The fence was promptly built and new flowers lovingly— and permanently—planted for the enjoyment of the entire community.

Mary Anna couldn't wait to tell Daniel how they had out-smarted Mr. Jones. He thoroughly enjoyed the story and it became a favorite tale, told around town for years.

The next day Mary Anna and Daniel were having coffee out on the shady side of the big porch. A big table had been put out there for breakfast. Mary Anna looked around the table, marveling at the swift passing of time.

Tump was married, and had come to stay overnight with his wife on their way into town. Molly was a lovely girl, and Mary Anna enjoyed watching the young couple bill and coo. Tump was very much like his father, and Mary Anna had a sense of deja vu as she watched them.

Peter had become a fine young man and would be a good rancher. He was sweet on Parcinda. There would be a wedding soon. Elizabeth, too, would marry soon. Mary Anna was proud of her daughter and her many musical accomplishments. Henry and Miss Florence were on their own place now. Willie was still pining for Miss Jackie. Oscar and Arthur were gangly colts. And then there was Annah, Mary Anna's reflection. Little Dan had taken over the care of Kate.

Mary Anna smiled at Daniel. "We're going to need more than one table this year for our Christmas feast."

Daniel felt every inch the patriarch of the clan. "The Lord is good." He took a bit of fluffy biscuit dripping with plum jam. "Did you think it would turn out like this?"

She looked at her husband. He had grown a beard and mustache. It was streaked with gray, but the eyes were still periwinkle blue, like her own. He was lean from his constant time in the saddle, but only a small spread across his girth spoke of his wealth.

"No," she admitted. "I never thought this far ahead. I spent most of my time worrying about what was going on right then. In the time I've had for reflection now, I am surprised to find myself no longer young. It seems like only yesterday I was eighteen, but when I look in the mirror or see our children, I still can't understand where the time has gone."

Oscar grinned hugely. "Arthur and I will be sixteen at the end of September."

"It's only August," she retorted fondly. "And don't get your hopes up about that big party. It isn't going to happen."

"Ah, Mama, we know about it already. You know how you like to show off your two handsome sons." He elbowed Arthur. "Maybe Rose will be there, huh?" Arthur turned scarlet. "I don't care if she is or not," he said loudly.

They scuffled a bit at the table until Daniel settled them down with a stern look. The boys were perfect halves of a whole. They had some sort of communication system between them no one could understand.

"I want you boys to ride the fences today," Daniel ordered them. "Take your pliers and tools to repair any breaks."

"Yes, sir."

"And watch for rattlers up on that rocky place. It's been a bad year for snakes. Take your rifles." Without a smile he added, "And if you kill any, don't bring home any skins. You boys don't need new belts."

The entire table broke out in laughter, and Henry turned the color of a beet. "Ah, Papa," he protested. "I was little then."

Mary Anna sent them out with a lunch big enough for three grown men. The day was oppressively hot, but riding pushed a cooling breeze across their tanned faces. They stopped at a place where the fence was down.

"Willie and Henry's trip to Anderson County sure was an adventure," said Arthur. "I wish I could have an adventure."

"Me, too. I wish I was going somewhere." Oscar sighed. "I love to hear the cowboys talk about the days when they made those drives."

"They're still doing the drives," Arthur said.

"Not the old way on this ranch. Papa has everything up to

date." He looked at his twin. "Besides we have to go to Huckabee Academy in the fall."

"I know. Mama and her schooling. But when we get out, let's go somewhere exciting. Maybe we could go to Anderson County."

"That doesn't sound exciting to me," Oscar said with disgust. "I'd rather go farther out west. Maybe to California. Now that would be an adventure."

One of the horses gave a frightened snort and a fast side step. Arthur grabbed the rifle and walked quickly toward the animals. He spotted the coiled rattler at once and shot his head off with a clean shot. "Nuisances. Worse than flies and mosquitoes."

"I hate those things," Oscar said with a shudder. "Papa said there was a man on the drive that used to eat them. Ugh."

They caught the jittery horses and moved on down the fence. Arthur looked up into the cloudless sky. "Sure is hot." He grinned. "There's a pool of water not too far from here. Maybe we ought to take a dip. Remember what Mama said about being careful. We might take a heatstroke out here in this hot sun. In fact, I feel one about come on right now. We'd better cool off."

"Art, you're bad," said his brother with a grin.

After their romp, they crawled onto the edge of the pool and lay back in the cool mud with their feet still in the water.

"You hungry, Art? I'm starving." Oscar walked to the horses, and took their lunch out of the saddlebags. They ate and agreed they should get on with their work. "I don't want a skinning by Papa," said Oscar.

Arthur grinned mischievously. "You know I'd never do anything to get us into trouble with him."

"Only every day of our lives," sighed Oscar.

They killed two more snakes that afternoon. The horses

were jumpy.

"Papa was right. The snakes are bad this year," Oscar said in a worried voice. "Be real careful where you put your feet," he ordered his brother.

"We'd better put on our chaps, too. Mine are so tough that no snake alive could get his fangs through that leather."

Oscar felt safer with his chaps on. He pulled on some work gloves, too. "I don't like snakes," he shot at his brother's unspoken remark.

"Did I say anything?" Arthur asked innocently.

"You didn't have to," Oscar answered. "I know you too well."

"I bet you don't know I stole a kiss from Jenny."

"Do, too. It was at the church picnic."

They laughed together, the two boys that knew each other's souls.

Suddenly Oscar's horse reared in panic. Oscar had been riding easy in the saddle with only the tips of his boots in the stirrup. The lunging movement of his horse threw him completely off the animal.

In a flash Arthur had his rifle out and killed the rattler coiled to strike. He ran over to his brother. "It's okay, I got him. You all right?"

Oscar didn't respond, and Arthur saw he'd been knocked unconscious by the fall. "Oscar! Oscar! Wake up! I got the snake." He put his hand under his brother's head and tried to raise it.

Oscar's eyes were wide open in surprise, but he didn't answer his brother's frantic plea.

"O, dear God, let him wake up. Mama'll kill me if you get hurt." He began crying and looking about him for help. "Help me, somebody, my brother's been hurt!" His voice echoed eerily across the land. He pulled Oscar up against him, cradling his head. "Oscar, say something to me! Please!"

Oscar's eyes stared at the scalding sky above. Arthur wept uncontrollably and rocked his brother's body. "Help," he whispered. "Help."

The sun was beginning to slide over to the west when he finally accepted the fact that no one could help him or Oscar. Awkwardly he draped Oscar's body over the saddle and led the horse at a slow walk toward home. "Oscar," he said, "you can't leave me. We have so much adventure planned. There's all those girls to kiss and the trips we want to make." He wiped at the dirty tears that stained his face with his hand. "I can't go home and tell Mama that you're dead. It'll kill her for sure. What am I going to do without you?" he wailed loudly to the silent sky.

Mary Anna was looking for the boys. Supper would be ready soon. It always irritated her when anyone was late for supper. She went outside and pounded loudly on the heavy iron triangle that was used to summon the men from the fields. "That ought to bring them fast enough," she said in an irate voice.

In the distance she could just make out two horses. "It's about time." But when she looked carefully, there was something wrong with the picture in her eyes. There was only one upright rider. "Daniel, come quick! One of the twins has been hurt!"

Daniel hurried out of the house. He saw Oscar across his saddle. "Get some water ready, Mary Anna."

She stood rooted to the spot. Her heart was pounding. *Don't let it be bad, God.* But when she saw the limp arms bumping against the side of the horse, her worst fears surfaced. She ran toward the boys with Daniel right behind her.

"It was a rattler, Mama! I killed him, but Oscar's hurt bad." Arthur said wildly.

Mary Anna helped Daniel lay the boy on the ground. As soon as she saw the wide-open eyes staring at nothing, she felt faint. She cradled Oscar's head in her lap. Arthur was babbling about the snake and how it had spooked the horses, but that he had killed the snake. Oscar should be all right.

Silently Daniel closed his dead son's eyes.

"Did the snake bite him?" she asked as her eyes scanned all his protective gear.

"No, I told you, I killed the snake. The fall knocked him unconscious. Make him wake up, Mama!" He was crying so hard Mary Anna had to listen carefully to understand him.

Oscar's head rolled unnaturally over her arm. Quietly she said, "His neck is broken." Blackness settled around her, cosseting her in numbness. "Take him in the house, Daniel." She leaned back as Daniel put his hands underneath the boy's inert form.

Mary Anna stood up and put her arms around Arthur. "He's not going to wake up, Arthur. He's dead. Come inside with me."

Arthur wept uncontrollably. "I tried to take care of him, Mama. I killed the snake. Killed a lot of them all afternoon. I tried so hard to make him wake up. I did the best I could."

Mary Anna led the weeping boy into the house. "I know you did, son, I know you did. You did fine," she said in a soothing voice. "You did everything you could. It's not your fault. It's going to be all right." She crooned softly to him as she had when he was a nursing baby and led him to the sofa in the front parlor. She sat beside him, holding him in her arms and rocking him.

Daniel came in quietly. His face was gray and strained. Tears had formed back behind his eyes, but they hadn't found a way out. He sat down heavily in a big rocking chair.

"What'll I do without him, Mama? We've never even spent

the night apart. He's always been there, just like half of me. What am I going to do?" Arthur sobbed. "I let my brother die. It was my fault. He was afraid of snakes. I should have seen it. I couldn't get him to wake up."

"Listen carefully, Arthur," said Mary Anna, "it wasn't your fault. It was an accident. You couldn't see the snake. The horse threw Oscar and broke his neck. There was no way you could wake him up. You did all the right things. It wasn't your fault," she repeated in a firm voice.

Annah, Little Dan, and Kate peered with fearful eyes around the door frame. "Come sit here with your brother," Mary Anna instructed them. "I'll be back in a minute." She left them sitting on either side of Arthur. Kate was holding his hand and Little Dan was patting his arm. Annah was in his lap nestled against him.

Mary Anna went up the stairs, pulling herself along the railing. She steeled herself for the next ordeal. Oscar was lying on his bed, looking for all the world as if he were sleeping quietly. She sat down on the edge of the bed and brushed back the hair on his forehead. He was cool to her touch. "My poor baby," she whispered. She took up his limp hand and held it in her own.

"Arthur is going to be only half a person for a long time until he gets used to your being gone," she told him. "I know you're with the Lord now, and that's a comfort for me." She felt the tears come unbidden and slide hotly down her face. She couldn't believe he was dead. None of her children had died after infancy. She had always kept death away with her nursing skills and the help of the Lord. She wanted to beg the Lord to give him back, to make a deal with him for Oscar's life.

The sound of boots on the staircase made her turn to see Tump and Peter, white-faced and red-eyed. She rose to accept their sad embraces.

"Oh, Mama, we're so sorry. For all of us." It was all Tump was able to get out. Peter was crying softly.

He took a deep breath and said, "I never thought it would be like this. I thought we'd all live and get old together."

Mary Anna nodded, but she said, "It's called life. The good times and the bad. You boys do your sorrowing for Oscar, but it's the living who need taking care of. Arthur is the one hurting the most. He's lost half of himself." She turned to look again on Oscar's face. "I want you to help me make him understand that it wasn't his fault. You must do this for me."

"We will, Mama, we promise," Peter said for both of them.

"Now go downstairs and stay with Arthur and send Elizabeth up here." Sadly she turned away to look again at Oscar. Elizabeth found her mother talking softly to Oscar. She choked back a sob. While Coleman and Rabbit made a coffin in the barn, Mary Anna and Elizabeth prepared Oscar's body for burial.

Molly and Parcinda made the house ready for the many visitors who were sure to start coming as the word spread. When Mary Anna entered the big parlor and saw Oscar laid out in his coffin, she felt a pain so overwhelming it almost knocked her to her knees. The ritual was so familiar: the coffin, the flowers, the quiet voices, the muffled sobbing. Food and friends began appearing, lavishing comfort and soft words.

My son is dead. She had to keep reminding herself of that fact. Everything was so unreal. But she knew her pain was equaled by Arthur's. She would need all her strength to get him through this ordeal. And Daniel needed her, too. He looked so old. Old and broken. He had always been so strong, but she knew this time she would have to be the strong one.

Daniel leaned heavily on her as they carried Oscar out to the cemetery, but he read the burial service with a strong voice. "A time for all things," she heard him say. "Today you shall be with me in paradise." The "ashes to ashes and dust to dust" made her heart hammer. She couldn't put a handful of soil on his coffin. She wouldn't. Before the men began to lower her son's coffin into the earth, Mary Anna abruptly turned around and headed for the house. "It's too much to bear," she cried as Daniel caught up with her.

Daniel's distraught face came close to hers, and through the mourning veil she heard him say, "This is the other side of the dream. We can't expect to have only the sweet. You've told me that. You've been afraid of losing one of the children. Now we have. But we can make it through this together. Even Jesus felt forsaken at one point. God will not make it all go away, but He will give us each day in which to recover. We haven't lost our whole family. We've unwillingly given Oscar back to his Maker. We can do this together with God's help. Hold on to me, Mary Anna. Hold on to me," he begged.

Mary Anna tried to look ahead. With a sudden, heart-wrenching realization, she knew that there could be others to bury unless she died in her footsteps right now. The ebb and flow of life, living, birthing, and dying undulated like the waves on the seashore. It was natural and normal. "But parents shouldn't have to bury their children," she whispered.

During the long days following the funeral, the entire family stayed together, never far from each other. They comforted and loved one another, suddenly aware of their own mortality. Life had become a precious thing, not something to be lightly frittered away.

Even Little Dan and Kate matured. Sometimes Mary Anna longed for them to fight and shout at each other. The peace and quiet of the house was not normal, and she wanted to hear the sounds of boots on the floors and doors banging and children talking loudly to each other.

Arthur was the one she watched. Even sleep held only night-mares of snakes and Oscar calling to him. Mary Anna moved him in with Willie. Gradually the paleness began to leave his face, and once in a while a small smile crossed his face.

The first milestone came at the end of September on the twin's birthdays. Mary Anna baked a coconut cake, the boys' favorite. She prepared their favorite meal: chicken fried steak and mashed potatoes with gravy. And she set a plate for Oscar in his usual place.

That night in the soft light, the family made an effort to celebrate Arthur's birthday. It was a strain on everyone.

Finally Arthur said, "I want to thank you for the good birthday. I know that Oscar is here with us tonight. He always loved a party." There was muffled laughter. "Mama and Papa, thank you for taking such good care of me and helping me to understand that it was an accident. I know that for sure now. I don't know why God took my brother, but I know he's okay and happy. I can feel it in my heart. And you know how Oscar and I always knew what the other was thinking." There was nodding and smiling.

"I'm glad Mama set a place for Oscar tonight. He will be with us, at least me, all the time. And I think it's time for all of us to quit being sad all the time. Life is like a river, and it's time for us to jump in and get scrubbed up for tomorrow. Tomorrow could be a wonderful day if we let it. Okay?" His young face begged for release from his sorrow and another chance to make things happy.

Mary Anna was openly crying, and Daniel had his napkin stuffed at his mouth. With glistening eyes the rest of the family smiled and gave Arthur the birthday present he really needed.

That night in the privacy of their big bed, Daniel said, "I

was so proud of Arthur tonight."

Mary Anna nodded in agreement. "He's right, you know. We do need to get on with life. I doubt a thousand deaths would make any one of our children's any easier, but I am peaceful about Oscar. He is with the Lord." She paused thoughtfully. "I wonder if the babies were there to welcome him?"

"Probably." Daniel pulled her a little closer to him as they cuddled under the covers. "Living out the dream did get hard there for a while. But you aren't sorry about us building a life out here, are you?"

"No. The story will be told no matter where we live. Are you sorry?"

"No," he admitted slowly. "I do wish I had the power to make nothing but good things happen, though."

"You wouldn't be happy with that arrangement, I'm sure," Mary Anna said firmly. "Life is a subtle blend of all shades of things. We've been so blessed so many times, I blush to think of all the good things the Lord has done for us. Oh, I ache to see Oscar come riding in with Arthur sometimes. But the pain is getting duller. And I look at the other children with different eyes now. I know they're not mine to keep. I can only take care of them and try to get them ready for their lives, whatever that may be."

She smiled. "That's been a bit of a relief, because I always thought it was up to me to keep them healthy and well and alive. Now I know I do the best I can, but I can't protect them from what I've been through. They would be only shells that would crumble at the first adversity. Our hard times have made us what we are. Their hard times will have to shape them, too."

And with those words, Mary Anna wrapped herself in her husband's embrace and was comforted.

ten

Of all Mary Anna's children, Annah was the most openly affectionate. It had been Annah who had done everything in her power to ease her mother's sorrow at Oscar's death. Annah had become the child of Mary Anna's heart.

She loved the same things Mary Anna did—the tender springtime, soft furry animals, babies—and she seemed to have an uncanny ability to sense the hidden thoughts and feelings of those around her.

Mary Anna was weeding the garden that went up the middle of the double walkways to the front door. The flowers were beginning to look beautiful, and it made her happy to see them flourish as her children had after Oscar's death a year ago.

Annah came out and helped her in the garden for a while. Carefully she pulled the weeds from the young plants. She had forgotten to bring her bonnet.

Mary Anna was tempted to order her seventeen-year-old daughter to put on a bonnet to keep her skin white, but she seemed so happy in the sunlight that Mary Anna was reluctant to spoil the time by mothering Annah. And her auburn hair looked alive and glowing. She was a beautiful young girl.

The mockingbird who lived in the oak trees close by sang his multiple songs of theft. The cicadas were whirring, and the horses neighed in the meadow. A bee buzzed Mary Anna's flowered bonnet on his way to the meadow flowers. As the rich smell of earth assailed her nose and she dug her hands into it's dampness, Mary Anna realized she had seldom felt such peace.

"Mama, will I fall in love?" Annah asked. "When I see Henry acting so dumb with Miss Florence, I wonder if that's love. Does love make you silly?"

Mary Anna laughed. "Sometimes I'm afraid it does."

"I don't want to fall in love then."

"I said sometimes. But love is a powerful force. Sometimes it makes people do things they never thought they could. I don't think dumb or silly is it's main definition."

"Did Papa make you feel silly?" She tried to see her mother's face up under her bonnet.

"No, but I did feel giddy when he was around. Sort of breathless sometimes. His just being there could make me tremble inside." Mary Anna's eyes turned inward as she remembered her short, intense courtship and early marriage.

"He must have been very handsome," Annah remarked.

"I think he still is. He's different, but still handsome."

"You're still pretty," Annah said candidly.

"Why, thank you, child. You know all the stories about knights in shining armor riding up to pretty maidens?" Mary Anna asked. "The thing I don't like about those stories is that happiness always comes at the end. The end of the story is only the beginning of the real, deep happiness. There's so much to learn about being married after the last page of those stories."

"Like what?"

"Like learning new things about each other even after you've been married for a long time. How to make each other happy. When to fight and when to walk away. What kind of father he'll be."

Annah paused in her digging and played with a long earthworm that was trying to get away from the bright sunlight. "I like the stories about the knights in shining armor, but I'm glad to know the story has a lot more to it. I never thought about what happens after they ride away together."

"Maybe to some people the married part is not as romantic as the courtship. And for some, I guess it isn't."

"But it has been for you and Papa. I can tell by your face." They exchanged broad smiles.

"I don't feel giddy around him now, but I still get a breathless feeling if he's been gone a while and I suddenly see him."

"I'll have to choose carefully and get a man like Papa."

"I doubt you could do much better," her mother agreed.

"I think I'd like to be married and have babies. When I see you and Papa together, sometimes when you don't think I'm looking, I see a special look pass between you. A secret look I've never seen you give anyone else."

"It's a married look, I suspect." She was surprised Annah could be so observant.

"If a man ever looks at me like that, I'll know he's the right one." Annah seemed to have decided on the answer to her own question.

They moved to the new rose garden that was Mary Anna's pride and joy. The flowers were fully blooming and gave unstintingly of their fragrance. Annah buried her face in one of the blooms and sighed deeply. "Nothing in the world smells as good as a rose," she said happily.

"And nothing is quite as thorny," her mother replied as she sucked her pricked finger.

"When I have a house, I'm going to have millions of roses all around it, so that no matter which way the wind blows, there will always be the smell of roses in the house."

"Some people take rose petals and glaze them with sugar."

"To eat?"

"It's supposed to be quite tasty. Maybe we should try it."

Annah pulled a petal from a deep red rose and nibbled on it. "It does have a sweet taste, but I don't think I'd like to eat very many of them. No," she decided, "roses belong in the garden, not on a table to be eaten."

Mary Anna clipped a few stems to put on the supper table. "I don't really like to cut the flowers. They live so much longer if you leave them on the bushes. But I do love to smell them. Once I had a little rose bead necklace. My mother made it for me. I haven't thought of that in years. She picked lots and lots of petals and put them in a black skillet with some spices and water. Then she rolled the mushed petals into little balls and put a pin through them until they dried. The balls were black, and she strung them on a string for me." Mary Anna fingered the roses she had cut. "I was so proud of that necklace. I wonder what happened to it? Funny how you can love something so much, and then it just disappears out of your life."

When they went in to cook supper, Annah took the roses from her mother, put them in a tall vase, and placed them on the table. "Roses mean happiness to me. They give so much of themselves, and they live only for our enjoyment."

Mary Anna put her arms around the girl and kissed the top of her head. "Some people are like that, too, my darling."

Annah smiled softly and hugged her mother back.

After supper Mary Anna hummed as she set her kitchen in order. It pleased her to have such luxury in which to work. Life had become as gentle as it could be on the frontier. She was just putting the freshly washed Blue Willow dishes back in their cupboard when Annah came in. She was limping.

"What's the matter, darling?"

"I stepped on an old nail out in the barn."

"Why weren't you wearing your shoes?" she fussed. "Let me see."

Obediently Annah sat down and put her injured foot up for Mary Anna's inspection. She wiped the bleeding surface clean. Annah winced as Mary Anna probed the wound with her finger.

"It looks deep. You say the nail was old?"

"Yes, real old. I know because it had rust on it."

Mary Anna's heart quickened in alarm, but she kept her face composed. "I'll need to clean it very carefully." She got out a basin and washed the wound with soap. Annah tried to be brave when she put the foot in a basin a second time to soak it in the strongest disinfectant Mary Anna had.

"It burns," she complained.

"I'm sorry, but we must get it as clean as possible." She smiled faintly. "Wouldn't do much good to fuss at you for being so careless at this point."

Annah wrinkled up her nose. "No, I really wasn't being careless, Mama. I was playing with the little kids. We were chasing each other and I jumped over this old lumber. Part of it fell off just as I stepped down. It was stacked right beside Old Molly's stall." Her glance scurried up to her mother's face in apology.

"Can't unspill the milk. But you just sit there a while until it's good and clean."

Mary Anna returned to her work with less joy in her heart. People could get very sick from wounds made by rusty nails—even die. Impatiently, she pushed the thought away.

Mary Anna silently inventoried her medicines. She watched Annah all evening for signs of fever and hid her worry from the girl. When Daniel came in to get a glass of buttermilk, she shared her anxiety with him out of Annah's hearing.

"You cleaned it well. She should be all right," he tried to reassure her, but she saw the worry in his eyes, too.

By the third day, the puncture was showing signs of swelling and the area was red despite soakings each morning and evening.

By lunch, Annah was feverish and grumpy. Mary Anna mixed up a tea of willow root to break the fever and applied cool, damp cloths to Annah's forehead.

In the days that followed, Annah's foot grew progressively worse. Her entire leg was swollen and red-streaked. Mary Anna continued cleaning the wound, but she knew it wasn't making Annah better. Her fever stayed high no matter what Mary Anna did.

In the night Daniel cradled Mary Anna in his arms. "Do you want to send to Ft. Worth for a doctor?"

"It would take too long, and she's too sick to take her

there." Stark fear colored her next words. "I don't think he could help her anyway." She knew there was no cure for the thing called lockjaw, and she cried herself into a short sleep. When she awoke, she spent long hours on her knees begging God to cure Annah. But the young girl continued her downward spiral.

Daniel stood in the doorway watching Mary Anna fight the desperate war against death. Her shoulders were stooped with fatigue as she bent over Annah to change the cloth. He could just hear the soft conversation between mother and daughter.

"Mama, am I going to die?" Annah's lips were dry and her voice raspy.

When Mary Anna didn't answer right away, she added, "I'm not afraid, Mama. You always said people go to heaven when they die, if they love Jesus."

"That's true." Mary Anna sat on the edge of the bed and took Annah's hand. She was encouraged by Annah's lucid conversation, but she had never lied to any of her children about anything. It was time to face the possibility. Mary Anna owed candid answers to Annah's question, to prepare her daughter for death.

"You are very sick, but I think you just need time to get well. It is also possible you may. . . ," she couldn't bring herself to say the word die, so she said, "not get well."

"I always thought it probably hurt to die. I don't hurt anywhere," she smiled. "Not even my foot."

"That's good." Mary Anna smoothed a confusion of curls from Annah's forehead, and the young girl gave her a wan smile.

"It's odd, but I'm not afraid I'll die at night. It's when I see the sun peeking up over the window sill that I'm scared. Like the sun is coming to get me. But if I can make it until noon, I've made it another day. And each day means one more to get well in." She sighed. "Look outside, Mama, the sun is still climbing." She grasped Mary Anna's hand more tightly. "It isn't twelve yet, is it?" she asked hopefully.

"Not yet, my love, but soon." Mary Anna wanted to throw herself over her daughter, hold on tightly, and scream out against this thing that was taking her child away a day at a time. She would help Annah hold off the morning by sheer will. Her strength would flow through Annah's hands, and together they would defeat the raid of the morning sun.

She held Annah's hand firmly in her own, and silently promised herself that every morning before dawn, she would come and help Annah. Together they could win. She held her tears in check as she begged the Ruler of the universe not to let Annah die. She didn't make foolish promises; she just begged.

"Mama, I feel better. Is it noon yet?"

Mary Anna looked back at Daniel who nodded yes. "Yes, it's noon." She steadied her voice. "You've made it another day, my sweet."

"Keep holding my hands. I feel so strong when you hold them." She closed her eyes, sighing, "What time is it?"

Daniel walked to the bedside, holding out his pocket watch for Mary Anna to see. "It's twelve-twenty. You made it, Annah."

Annah smiled a long, slow smile. "Yes, I did. Twelve-twenty." Her head fell gently to the side as she let out her last breath.

"No!" cried Mary Anna. "No! Annah! It's twelve-twenty! You made it!" She looked helplessly at Daniel, who stood with tears running freely down his face to nestle in his soft beard. He knelt down beside the bed and sobbed into the colorful quilt.

"No, no," Mary Anna whispered numbly. "It's twelve-twenty." The refrain echoed in her head, rolling like a moan in a ghostly fog.

Daniel raised his head to look on the peaceful face of his dead child. "Oh, Annah," he whispered brokenly, "my sweet Annah." He leaned against Mary Anna and wrapped his arms around her, rocking her for both their comfort.

Mary Anna looked at her white-knuckled hands still holding tightly to her daughter's limp fingers.

Elizabeth appeared at the door. One glance told the story. White-faced with grief, she went to her parents. "Come away. I'll take care of her. Come away." She took her mother's hand from Annah's and got both her parents on their feet, guiding them downstairs. "Rest now. I'll take care of everything."

Daniel took Mary Anna to their bedroom and helped her stretch out on their bed. She was dazed and her hands were like ice. He spread the Double Wedding Ring quilt over her and sat down in the rocking chair where he could watch. Her face was composed, but tears ran unabated from her blue eyes onto her pillow.

He rocked until she closed her eyes, checked her carefully, and then sat back down in the rocker. Unreality was his shield from the pain that had first washed over him. *Elizabeth will take care of Annah,* he thought. And he rocked.

Molly helped Elizabeth bathe and dress Annah's body. Both women wept silently as they put her in her best white dress and combed her hair. Then Elizabeth used a pair of scissors to clip some of Annah's hair in the back where it wouldn't show. Later it would be woven into a lovely flower shape and framed.

Tump and Peter, in silent shock, sent for the neighbors. In a short time, men were fashioning a wooden coffin in the barn and solemn-faced women were bringing in food. It had been only fourteen months since they had done this for Oscar's funeral.

The casket was lined with white cloth placed over a bedding of wooden shavings, and the outside was draped with black cloth to cover the unfinished wood. Wooden sawhorses were set up in the main room, and the casket placed on it. The sawhorses were hidden with more black cloth.

Tenderly Annah was carried downstairs by Tump and placed inside the coffin. Elizabeth put a fresh rosebud in her sister's clasped hands. A tear fell from Elizabeth's face and watered the fragrant flower.

The family took turns sitting with Annah's body through the long night.

In the morning, Mary Anna, dressed in a stark black dress, hat, and mourning veil, was led by Daniel to view Annah's body, but it was apparent to all that she had retreated to a place where her pain and grief couldn't reach her. She sat where they put her, never uttering a sound. Only the tears that ran down her drawn face were alive. The rest of her benumbed body was as dead as Annah.

Later that morning, the family joined their neighbors at

the small church. Mary Anna sat in the front pew beside Daniel. Her heart lurched in painful awareness as she saw the coffin a few feet from where she sat. For a moment she thought the blackness would engulf her again as she smelled the heavy perfume of the roses that surrounded the coffin. Annah lay with an expression of peacefulness, one red rose-bud placed in her white hands.

Mary Anna felt faint, and a clammy sweat broke out on her forehead. Daniel was squeezing her hand hard. Annah looked so calm that for one insane moment Mary Anna was positive she would sit up from her sleep and smile, wondering what all the fuss was about.

Mary Anna longed to take away the heavy black veil from her face. There was little air in the room, and she felt faint again. Her mind wandered around, helpless to focus on the real reason for her being here. Muffled sobs rippled through the small building, and she tried to remember why someone would be crying. Annah couldn't possibly be dead. *Why, just look at her. She's just sleeping*. She heard a male voice say that very thing, and felt Daniel shudder with his grief. The voice rolled on and on, saying things that didn't register in her mind. All she could feel was the awful blackness waiting at the edge of her consciousness to enfold her in its arms and the smell of roses hanging heavily in the hot summer air.

And then she was walking, Daniel supporting her wavering step toward the cemetery. She saw the raw hole in the earth and realized they were going to put Annah in that hole. *No, no*, her heart screamed, *don't cover her up like that, she'll smother!*

But it was done, and the roses spread in a colorful shroud over the dark earth. Mary Anna held one of the roses in her hand and looked in surprise where the thorn had dug into her hand and blood was staining her black glove. But she couldn't unclasp her hand to stop it. Nothing in her body was working properly. Strange hands had taken away her child and put her in the earth. Now strange hands were guiding her away from that earth.

Vaguely she heard Virginia say something to her. Mary Anna could see her lips moving, but the words made no sense. Daniel said something to her, but he seemed to be speaking from the bottom of a well. She tried to concentrate. He was saying something important. His face looked lined and old. *He's so sad. What has happened to make him so sad? It must be terrible.* And then the smell of roses threw her back into the blackness. Annah was dead. That's why he looked so sad. She longed to reach out and embrace him, to comfort him, but her arms were like dead sticks. Something hard and white hot had risen in her chest. The ache was almost unbearable, and to her surprise, she found tears falling on the rose still clutched in her hand. Someone tried to take the rose, but she held on tightly. It was her only hold on life now. The only thing that was real in this upside-down world. Desperately she tried to form the words that would send a prayer to the Lord, but her mind remained blank.

It was getting dark. Someone had removed her mourning veil, and she heard soft footsteps and hushed voices around her. The bitter taste of a medicinal tea burned her lips. She pushed the glass away and felt hands leading her to her bedroom.

She was so tired. So tired. As she stretched out on the soft mattress, the feathers cradled her gently. Then she remembered Annah sleeping on the soft mattress of death. There was no sound, but Mary Anna felt the hot tears rushing down the side of her face into her hair and pillow. It was hot outside, but she felt as cold as ice. Fatigue pulled at her, and the blackness beckoned, inviting and painless. She gave herself up to its greedy arms with only the smell of roses to accompany her down its ebony path.

Every now and then she surfaced to a level just below reality. She was aware of people and voices, Daniel's most of the time. But even her deep love for him couldn't coax her to give up this new love that kept her. It was her friend and lover, stroking and caressing her in its arms of forgetfulness. It whispered to her to stay away from the light. The light brought only pain and sorrow, and she embraced the blackness, giving herself to it completely.

She was dreaming of being with Annah in a garden tending the roses. Annah was beautiful and happy. But from beyond the garden someone was crying and calling to Mary Anna.

"Mama, please don't die! Please come back to me!" It was the voice of a small child. She looked at Annah, but Annah was smiling. Mary Anna let herself go toward the light carefully. When she opened her eyes, Kate was standing beside her bed, crying.

The child's face was frightened and sad. Mary Anna looked back at Anna and saw her smile gently. Then Annah raised her hand in a slow wave of farewell. She looked so radiant that Mary Anna didn't mind leaving the garden for a moment to take care of the crying child.

Kate crawled up into bed with Mary Anna and lay with her head on her mother's breasts. Mary Anna took the child in her arms and stroked her hair. Annah was still smiling and waving at her, but she seemed to be moving away from Mary Anna.

"What's the matter, Kate? Do you want to play in the garden with Annah, too? You'd better hurry."

The child cried harder, and Mary Anna knew this was not what Kate wanted. She pulled the child closer and kissed her wet cheeks. "What do you want, darling?"

"Don't go away from me," she sobbed. "I need you."

"I'm right here. I won't leave you." She felt the soft texture of Kate's hair underneath her stroking hand.

"Hold me, Mama. Hold me."

Big blue eyes, freshly washed with tears, pleaded with Mary Anna. Thunder cracked across the sky. "Don't be afraid of the storm," Mary Anna soothed her young daughter. "It won't hurt you. Come on, we'll get some milk and cookies. That always makes you feel better." Slowly she sat up and led the child into the kitchen, feeling the small hand clutching her own.

Kate sat down obediently at the table. "I'll get both of us some cookies and milk, and we'll listen to the angels bowl." Mary Anna sat down at the table and shared the food with Kate. "That's what my father said was happening when it thundered," she reassured the child. "The angels were bowling."

Daniel came hurrying into the kitchen.

"Do you want some milk and cookies too?" asked Mary Anna. She accepted his embrace and the soft kiss on her forehead.

"Yes, I'd like some. I'm glad to see you up," he said carefully.

"I've been asleep a long time, I think."

"Yes," he agreed. "It's been a long time. I've missed you."

She was surprised to see tears in his eyes. "It must have been a long while. You've gotten quite gray, my dear. I will be careful not to sleep that long again."

One by one the family members joined the big table and had the offered milk and cookies. They were watching her carefully.

And then she remembered the dream. "I was just in the garden with Annah. As I woke up, she was waving good-bye to me." She looked levelly at Daniel. "Annah is dead, isn't she? That's why I slept so long."

"Yes," he answered in a choked voice. "Annah is dead. But the rest of us are still here and we love and need you."

"I'll be all right now. I saw her in the garden and she was very happy. I can leave her now. She's happy."

As she grew stronger, Mary Anna accepted Annah's death, and the tearing pain lessened. Only the smell of roses occasionally made her gasp. And then she went with Daniel down to put roses on Oscar and Annah's graves. She was calm, for she had seen with her own eyes how radiant Annah was, and she tried to comfort Daniel with her knowledge. She seldom went to the grave as the days faded into the winter months. There was no need. Annah wasn't there.

Mary Anna looked at each of her children with new eyes as she had after Oscar's death. Their life was a slender golden thread suspended between heaven and earth. The thread could be broken at any moment, and she counted precious the days that she could have them. Yet she took comfort in knowing exactly where they would go if the time came again to give up one of them.

Daniel is not the only one who is gray-haired, she noted as she brushed her long hair. With sorrow and wisdom had come the confirming streaks of gray. She twisted her hair into a soft knot on the top of her head with fingers made deft from years of practice. Her clothes were too large for her, but her appetite had returned.

She heard the gentle squeak of the front porch swing and went outside to join Daniel. "It's still beautiful weather for October, isn't it?" he said.

"Yes. I love looking at the trees in their fall finery."

They spoke of soft, gentle things, edging their way back to one another.

Mary Anna looked at Daniel with careful eyes. They were still young in their hearts and minds, but Mary Anna was fifty-one and Daniel was already fifty-five years old. God willing, there would be many more years left for them together.

She laid her hand on Daniel's strong brown one, resting in his lap. Turning slightly, she looked at his face with great love and deep affection. "Remember when we were talking about living out the dream, and I told you I was afraid of it sometimes?"

"Yes." He patted her hand and then lovingly placed a kiss on its palm.

"These were the times I was afraid of. We were living in an impossibly happy time when everything was going right. I knew it couldn't always be that way. Money can't protect you from the realities of life. But God can get you through those times of sorrow." Softly she added, "I wouldn't have left you, you know. I was tempted because the pain was so great," she admitted.

"I wasn't sure if you would come back to me. I know that Annah was the child of your heart, a miniature of you in every way. It's all right that you loved her the best of our children. I was only praying you didn't love her more than you loved me."

She smiled sadly at that. "No, I could never love the children more than I love you. I needed time to heal. And my need was so great that only God could be of comfort to me at the time. Maybe that's why I had to give her back to the Lord. It won't be my ultimate test, Daniel. With clear eyes I can see what it will be like to lose you, if you die before I do." Her voice was strong and controlled. "I may have to walk through that darkness again, but I know I can do it." She dropped her gaze to the floor of the porch, embarrassed to admit the next thought to him. "I'm selfish, for I hope I die before you do. I don't want to have to face life without you."

"We have eight living children of the thirteen you've borne, grandchildren, a good reputation, a beautiful ranch and farm, and each other. We have survived almost everything together building the dream. And we're still living the dream. God has given us these years in which to hold the dream in our hands, realize it, live it, and pass it on to our children. No man or woman could ask for more."

She leaned against him as the slow rhythm of the swing rocked them. "No matter what happens from now on, I won't be afraid. I've seen that dream fulfilled. And I see many more years of it yet to come. Thank You, Lord," she whispered. "Thank You."

epilogue

On May 7, 1977, a historical marker, duly authorized by the Texas Congress, was erected in the cemetery where Daniel and Mary Anna are buried:

Daniel Robert Thornton (1833-1911) and Mary Anna (Garland) Thornton (1837-1906). D. R. Thornton from Mississippi married Mary Anna, Daughter of frontier fighter, Peter Garland, in Anderson County, Texas, in 1853. The Thorntons settled here in 1857 as cattle raisers, and helped make this frontier safe for less hardy settlers. The couple reared eight children. Thornton, a confederate soldier in the Civil War (1860s), served as a County Commissioner (1876-78), and gave land for local school (1882). Hannibal Cemetery stands on the donated land (1976).

The cemetery is located eighteen miles northwest of Stephenville, two miles off SH108 on County Road. Barton Springs was renamed Hannibal.

On that hot May day, Thornton descendants from all over Texas assembled to pay homage to their forebearers. My mother, Fern Thornton Tinian, had the honor of unveiling the historical marker.

At the close of the ceremony, someone casually mentioned the old log cabin was still standing. I was astonished, for I thought of that cabin as being a thousand years old and long destroyed.

It wasn't in the best of shape, but it still stood, solidly built, and gaping here and there where a log was gone. I touched the weathered logs in an effort to feel the words they had stored, conversations of long ago captured by time.

Mary Anna and Daniel had built and lived in this very cabin. Incredible! When I walked around to the back, I could see a faint path still leading to a small stream.

I had gone to the dedication service more to please my parents than from a sense of honoring Daniel and Mary Anna. I knew nothing about them. When Mother spoke fondly of "Steamville," it stirred no memories in me. But now I stood with my hand touching the past. The cabin was slowly being bumped down by the cattle that pastured there. Ironic that it would be the cattle, not the Indians, who destroyed it.

I saw the cabin disappearing forever and couldn't bear the thought. My husband, Mel, didn't argue when I begged him to put one of the smaller loose logs in our car. I pulled out a heavy pink-tinted slab of limestone from the foundation. He did balk when I said I wanted the door to make a table. "We only have a station wagon—and four kids," he reminded me. I think he envisioned the entire cabin being loaded by nightfall. Today the log is a long stool, thanks to my friend, Jim Deal. On it sits a framed picture of the 1904 Thornton family portrait and underneath it, the foundation stone.

It has been a joyful labor of love to get to know Mary Anna and Daniel and to share their lives. Many years have passed since my fingers touched that building, sealing me forever into the lives of my great great-grandparents. I'm eternally grateful for the memories they left behind.

A Letter To Our Readers

Dear Reader:

In order that we might better contribute to your reading enjoyment, we would appreciate your taking a few minutes to respond to the following questions. When completed, please return to the following:

Rebecca Germany, Managing Editor
Heartsong Presents
P.O. Box 719
Uhrichsville, Ohio 44683

1. Did you enjoy reading *Dreams Fulfilled*?
   ❏ Very much. I would like to see more books
      by this author!
   ❏ Moderately
      I would have enjoyed it more if _____
      _____

2. Are you a member of **Heartsong Presents**? ❏Yes ❏No
   If no, where did you purchase this book? _____
   _____

3. What influenced your decision to purchase this
   book? (Check those that apply.)

   ❏ Cover   ❏ Back cover copy
   ❏ Title   ❏ Friends
   ❏ Publicity   ❏ Other_____

4. How would you rate, on a scale from 1 (poor) to 5
   (superior), the cover design? _____

5. On a scale from 1 (poor) to 10 (superior), please rate the following elements.

  ___Heroine ___Plot

  ___Hero   ___Inspirational theme

  ___Setting ___Secondary characters

6. What settings would you like to see covered in **Heartsong Presents** books?_____

_____

_____

7. What are some inspirational themes you would like to see treated in future books?_____

_____

_____

8. Would you be interested in reading other **Heartsong Presents** titles? ❑ Yes ❑ No

9. Please check your age range:
 ❑ Under 18 ❑ 18-24 ❑ 25-34
 ❑ 35-45   ❑ 46-55 ❑ Over 55

10. How many hours per week do you read? _____

Name _____

Occupation _____

Address _____

City_____ State_____ Zip_____

Colleen L. Reece
Anita Corrine Donihue

This special gift book is a treasury of holiday stories, reminiscences, ideas, prayers, poetry, recipes, and more! Bring the joy of the holiday season into your home with traditions you can make your own as you celebrate the joy of Christ's birth with your family and friends.

64 pages, Hardbound, 5" x 6 ½"

Send to: Heartsong Presents Reader's Service
P.O. Box 719
Uhrichsville, Ohio 44683

Please send me _____ copies of *Joy to the World*. I am enclosing **$5.97 each** (please add $1.00 to cover postage and handling per order. OH add 6.25% tax. NJ add 6% tax.). Send check or money order, no cash or C.O.D.s, please. **To place a credit card order, call 1-800-847-8270.**

NAME _____

ADDRESS _____

CITY/STATE _____ ZIP _____

······Heart♥ng ······

Any 12 *Heartsong* Presents titles for only $26.95 ★★

★★plus $1.00 shipping and handling per order and sales tax where applicable.

HISTORICAL ROMANCE IS CHEAPER BY THE DOZEN!

Buy any assortment of twelve *Heartsong* Presents titles and save 25% off of the already discounted price of $2.95 each!

HEARTSONG PRESENTS TITLES AVAILABLE NOW:

(If ordering from this page, please remember to include it with the order form.)

·············Presents ··········

Great Inspirational Romance at a Great Price!

Heartsong Presents books are inspirational romances in contemporary and historical settings, designed to give you an enjoyable, spirit-lifting reading experience. You can choose wonderfully written titles from some of today's best authors like Peggy Darty, Colleen L. Reece, Tracie J. Peterson, VeraLee Wiggins, and many others.

When ordering quantities less than twelve, above titles are $2.95 each.

Heartsong Presents
Love Stories Are Rated G!

That's for godly, gratifying, and of course, great! If you love a thrilling love story, but don't appreciate the sordidness of some popular paperback romances, **Heartsong Presents** is for you. In fact, **Heartsong Presents** is the *only inspirational romance book club*, the only one featuring love stories where Christian faith is the primary ingredient in a marriage relationship.

Sign up today to receive your first set of four, never before published Christian romances. Send no money now; you will receive a bill with the first shipment. You may cancel at any time without obligation, and if you aren't completely satisfied with any selection, you may return the books for an immediate refund!

Imagine. . .four new romances every four weeks—two historical, two contemporary—with men and women like you who long to meet the one God has chosen as the love of their lives. . .all for the low price of $9.97 postpaid.

To join, simply complete the coupon below and mail to the address provided. **Heartsong Presents** romances are rated G for another reason: They'll arrive *Godspeed!*
